Starwinders:
Nohana's Triangles

Tyree Campbell

Starwinders 2: Nohana's Triangles
by Tyree Campbell

All rights reserved. No part of this book may be reproduced or transmitted in any form or by any means, electronic or mechanical, including photocopying or recording or by any information storage and retrieval systems, without expressed written consent of the author and/or artists.

Starwinders 2: Nohana's Triangles is a work of fiction. Names, characters, places, and incidents are products of the author's imagination. Any resemblance to actual events or persons, living or dead, is entirely coincidental.

Story copyright owned by Tyree Campbell
Cover illustration "Eyrie Rescue" by Laura Givens
Cover design by Laura Givens

First Printing, May 2024

Hiraeth Publishing
P.O. Box 1248
Tularosa, NM 88352
e-mail: hiraethsubs@yahoo.com

Visit www.hiraethsffh.com for online science fiction, fantasy, horror, scifaiku, and more. Stop by our online bookstore for novels, magazines, anthologies, and collections. **Support the small, independent press...and your First Amendment rights.**

Also by Tyree Campbell

Nyx Series (Novels):
Nyx: Malache
Nyx: Mystere
Nyx: The Protectors
Nyx: Pangaea
Nyx: The Redoubt

Yoelin Thibbony Rescues (Novels)
The Butterfly and the Sea Dragon *
The Moth and the Flame *
The Thursday Child*
Avatar

Lark Series (Novels)
The Desert Lark
The Iphajean Lark
The Justice Lark
The Traffic Lark
The Illusion Lark

Novels:
The Adventures of Colo Collins &
Tama Toledo in Space and Time
The Adventures of Colo Collins &
Tama Toledo in Love and in Trouble
Aoife's Kiss
The Breathless Stars
The Dice of God
The Dog at the Foot of the Bed
The Dog at War
The Gifted
Indigo

Iuliae: Past Tense
The Protocol
The Quinx Effect
Starwinders: Nohana's Heart
Starwinders: Nohana's Triangles
Thuvia, Maid of Earth
A Wolf to Guard the Door
The Woman from the Institute

Superheroine Novellas:
Bombay Sapphire 1 **
Bombay Sapphire 2 **
Bombay Sapphire 3 **
Bombay Sapphire 4 **
Bombay Sapphire 5
Oliva Sudden 1
Peridot 1
Peridot 2
Peridot 3
Peridot 4
Voyeuse 1
Voyeuse 2
Voyeuse 3

Collections:
AbracaDrabble
Drink Before the War
A Nice Girl Like You
(published by Khimairal, Inc)
Quantum Women *

Novellas:
Becoming Jade
Cloudburst
Future Tense
The Girl on the Dump
The Martian Women
Sabit the Sumerian
Sarrow

Poetry Collections
A Danger to Self and Others

SF for Younger Readers
Pyra and the Tektites 1
Pyra (graphic novel) 1
Pyra and the Tektites 2
Pyra (graphic novel) 2
Pyra and the Tektites 3
Pyra and the Tektites 4
Pyra and the Tektites 5
Pyra and the Tektites 6

* published by Nomadic Delirium Press
** published by Pro Se Press

All titles are available from the Shop at
www.hiraethsffh.com

For Alan Ira Gordon, who loves adventure...

"It is impossible for someone to love someone wholeheartedly without loving all people somewhat."
~ adapted from Robert A. Heinlein's *The Notebooks of Lazarus Long*

Part I: Experience

001: Point of Contention

The rock in the cliff had been too friable for Cahill and Nohana to climb by driving pitons into it. To rescue the infant, they had elected to descend by ropes secured to the top of the peak, and eventually to reach the ground three hundred meters below by rappelling. Nohana might have attempted the rescue solo, except that she could not hold the infant and simultaneously fend off the attacks from the cliff harpies and maintain her braking ability. Cahill had volunteered to provide protection.

"Don't look down," he called out, dangling in the breeze two meters away.

Nohana fumed. "You keep saying that. Vertigo is the least of my concerns."

She allowed herself to drop another five meters, which brought her almost to the level of the nest. Her boot-clad feet caught at the lip of the opening. She bent a little to peer inside. A few strands of light brown hair obscured her vision, blown there by a gust of wind that now swayed her on the rope, and she quickly brushed them away on the rope.

"Can you see anything?" Cahill asked.

Bending further, she glanced down at the ground. She had just reduced the potential fall to two hundred ninety-five meters. She doubted the lost five meters would make much difference. Easing the gloved grip of her brake hand, she dropped another meter.

Inside the opening, the predator parents had constructed a great nest of twigs, grass, leaves, river detritus, clots of offal, and picked bones. In the middle slept three brown cliff harpy nestlings and one sepia-skinned infant in a soiled diaper. The little boy was so far inside the nesting area that she would have to crawl in to retrieve him. Despite puncture wounds in the legs where the harpy's talons had clutched him, he was still breathing.

"I see enough," she said. "It'll take me a minute or two to reach—"

"Here they come," yelled Cahill.

"Keep them off me."

She dropped another meter, got her footing, and spilled herself inside on her hands and knees. The impact awakened the infant. It also elicited a squawked cry from one of the nestlings that was sure to add incentive to the parents. Dried bones jabbed at her as she crawled closer. The smell of offal and spoiled meat assailed her nostrils, and she fought her gorge back down. The baby was squalling now, and she saw pain in his dark blue eyes as she scooped him up. As she eased back out of the nest, something landed a hard blow on her rump. She felt needles pierce her skin. The wounds stung; it was difficult to shunt the pain aside, into an unused dark corner of her mind, where she might examine it later at her leisure.

"Pol! Get it off me!"

A hook raked her back, but still she clutched the infant in the crook of one arm and held the brake with the other hand. A hard blow landed, just at her left hip, freeing her momentarily from the predatory attack. She spilled out into the open air, swaying with the gust of wind, desperately clutching the baby.

A harpy dove at her and missed, catching its wing in the rope, which now twisted in the wind. Unable to stabilize herself, she kicked out at the cliff, throwing herself further away from it. When she swung back, she blocked her momentum with her legs and feet, and for a moment she was still.

A harpy struck Cahill, and he lost his brake, regaining it after plunging ten meters. There, he was no good to her as protection, unless he fired his Krupp—something Nohana did not wish him to do. Although she was not yet fully stabilized, she loosened her brake grip and slid down to his level. Above her, the cliff harpies landed in their nest to check on their young.

Dripping blood and sweat, and gasping for breath, Nohana plummeted down the cliff, braking intermittently.

So tightly did she hold the squalling infant that when she reached the ground, Ayvy had to pry him free. A moment later, Cahill landed beside Nohana.

A dark woman in mobcap and peasant garb came running to them. Taking the infant from Ayvy, she wept as she offered profuse thanks. After she dashed off again, Ayvy said, to Nohana, "It's worse than it looks. You're going to need skin patches."

"And something for the sting," Nohana muttered.

As she collapsed into Cahill's arms, she heard Ayvy instruct Freya, the *Black Ice* computer, to downdock. The echoes of the name of their destination, Gingham Dog, faded as Nohana passed out.

***

The Unit, they called themselves, a troika and frequent *ménage à trois*, a disparate triad. Ayvy was Angrboda Vigdisdottir, sought for the murder of her pastfather. Pol Cahill, a former operative of Confederation Security who had refused orders to kill a woman, was now sought for aiding and abetting a fugitive and for assault on a security official. And Nohana...

Only two months earlier, at eighteen, Nohana had pleaded with the other two to take her along with them, take her from Cullen's Lode and show her the stars. The green star with rays that was tattooed on her left shoulder declared Nohana to be fully an adult, having been guided into educational, social, and sexual maturity, able to make choices and decisions that were appropriate on Cullen's Lode, but sometimes met with disapproval or contumely on other worlds. It was she who had declared the triangle of their association and their inter-relationships to be equilateral. Ayvy, who had hoped for companions in her vague quest to do good with her substantial finances, and Cahill, remaking himself after a self-imposed seclusion, found Nohana's triangle to be what they wanted...and needed.

The stability of the emerging triangle fluctuated at first. Ayvy, accustomed to position, tried to impose too much direction on Cahill, who was accustomed to independence of action, and resented her for it. Nohana proved to be the unifier, listening to both sides without judgment, which made it easy to talk with her, and ultimately with each other.

All of this came to a head five days after Nohana was taken on board, when Ayvy's plan to hijack a shipment of gold ingots came to fruition. They came out of it with gold and each other. Following a few nights on a beach on Cullen's Lode, following bawdy ballads, good ale, intense intimacies, and quiet moments of introspection, they went out into a milieu whose leadership and officials were looking to imprison them forever and a day and whose peoples needed someone now and then to lend them a hand.

Thus, the Unit.

***

En route to Gingham Dog, Nohana regained consciousness. She felt as if she had been assembled from cheap tape and baling wire. The physical and emotional cost of rescuing the infant from the harpies left her limp in body and spirit. She saw Ayvy's face hovering over her, and long strands of Ayvy's soft yellow hair caressed her skin.

"Pol?" she asked.

"On the bridge," Ayvy told her. "I'm not going to ask how you feel."

Nohana gave a feeble nod, and drew the tip of her tongue over cracked lips. "Saves words," she murmured.

"The recike got the blood out of your denims. Next time wear black instead of blue; the bloodstains are less noticeable. And your jersey is irreparable." She paused. "Nohana."

"Uh-oh."

Ayvy laughed, but quickly sobered. "No, you did a great job. But I should have gone instead. I have experience. There was no need to insist that we draw lots."

Her tone dulled. "How do I get experience?" she asked.

"Yeah. How?" She looked up at the stateroom commo, though it was unnecessary to do so. "Freya, time to Gingham Dog?"

"Five minutes seven seconds, Your Highness."

"Doctor Margle will send out a gurney."

"I'll walk," said Nohana. "I have experience in that."

Jero Margle escorted Nohana into his examination room, and did not question the presence of Cahill when she bared her wounds. Margle's round face was grim, and within seconds the medical whites encasing his round body were stained with fresh blood. His gray eyes fought to be impartial as he examined her, emitting a "Hmm..." with disturbing regularity.

"Cliff harpy, you say." Finished with the preliminary, he straightened up from her. "I'm not familiar with that particular species, although I can well imagine it. We'll have to assume that the talons were caked with decayed organic matter, some of which is now under your skin. Each puncture has to be cleansed thoroughly and disinfected. And those bites on your back as well. I'm sorry, my dear, but this is going to hurt. I can anesthetize you, or give you something good for the pain."

"I think I'd rather have something bad for the pain," she said, and cracked a wan smile.

"I do recommend a mild anesthetic," Margle told her. "You'll be awake and aware, but you might as well be reading a book."

"All right. You're my doctor."

"And you're my patient. If you'd rather nobody watched except the nurse who'll assist me, I'll shoo them out."

Nohana shook her head, and threw a quick glance at Ayvy. "No, I want the full experience. You never know when it might be useful."

Ayvy tagged Cahill on the arm. "Let's go grab a coffee," she said. "Jerry will let us know when he's done."

"You go on ahead."

Taut, her lips paled. "Suit yourself," she said, and departed.

In the break room, Ayvy sat sullen. The shots from Nohana regarding experience had bitten her to the quick, more so because they were unexpected and uncharacteristic of her. It couldn't be cramps or associated discomfort, for Nohana had had her shot for menstrual suppression, and would not endure the monthlies until she chose to by taking a counter-shot. No, it had to be something else. But what?

Ayvy sipped her coffee, and tried not to consider the spat. Often an insight came when she had ceased searching for it. But on this occasion nothing came to her. She checked the time on the Palmetto. Margle had been working on her for half an hour. She wished now she had not departed so stiffly or abruptly, but it was too late to make amends for that. To return now was tantamount to surrender, and she had no idea what she was yielding to.

Just after she refilled her cup, Cahill entered the break room. She looked up at him expectantly, hoping for an update without having to request it. He said nothing as he prepared his own cup and sat down across the table from her.

"Well?" said Ayvy at last.

Undisguised reluctance tightened his face. "Jerry and Thoma are still working on her," he replied, and sipped his coffee as if to avoid speaking further.

"How much longer?"

Again Cahill hesitated. "I didn't ask," he said, and took some more coffee. With the cup now half-full, he got up and started to walk away.

"What did I do?" she called out. "Pol, what did I say?"

Head inclined, he came to a stop, and considered. Finally he turned back around and reseated himself. "You sat on her," he said.

"What? I did what?"

"You are denying her the opportunity to grow."

"I'm denying her the opportunity to die!"

"She would have died willingly, if that had been what it took to save that baby," he told her. "You weren't there. You didn't see the concentration in her face as she fought the rope and the wind and the harpies, to hold on tightly to that infant and keep her brake intact so she wouldn't plummet. And the terrible thing about the rescue is that woman probably will leave the baby alone out in the open again while she does her laundry or cooks or whatever distracts her from her primary focus. People don't learn, they don't make the necessary adjustments in their actions or thoughts, not right away. Sometimes it never occurs to them that the problem is internal."

Ayvy glared at him. "You mean me. You're talking about me."

He drew a deep breath and slowly exhaled, steadying himself. "Ayvy, I love you dearly. I love Nohana dearly. But since the gold hijack you've generally behaved like a mother songbird who refuses to allow her fledglings to fly. We didn't form this Unit just to do some good somewhere. We also formed it for the relationships, to love and nurture one another."

"She's only—"

"Seventeen. Eighteen now. I know. That was my argument before, and I lost it completely. She's a woman. She's fighting to—"

"You say that as if you think she's more woman than I am."

"Oh, for goddesses' sake, Ayvy!"

But upon rising she had spilled her coffee and was already headed for the door and the exit.

002: There Will I Follow

After Thoma wheeled a woozy Nohana to the recovery room, Cahill sat in Margle's office and waited while the doctor changed clothes in front of him. Finished, Margle perched a hip on a front corner of his desk and brought him up to date.

"That sealant will grow new skin over the gashes in her back," he began, ticking points off on his fingers. "If there are scars, they'll be so faint as to go unnoticed except by close," he cleared his throat, "very close examination."

"I've had a sealant or two, myself."

"I noticed that the last time you were here. Next point is that the talon punctures are now innocuous. Again, no or almost no scarring. A couple hours a day under a gentle sun for four or five days should develop a seamless tan. That green star tattoo tells me she's from Cullen's Lode. If memory serves, there's an abundance of beaches."

"Yeah. Wish I was on one now."

Margle nodded. "Which brings me to my final point. I don't know what has raised Ayvy's hackles, and I'm not really trained in relationship counseling, but if you and/or she need to talk..."

"She left Gingham Dog about two hours ago."

His face fell. "I feared as much."

"I'm open to advice, Doctor."

"Jerry. Please." He slid further up on his desk and sat comfortably. "I've known Ayvy since her second year at university. I'm not going to talk out of turn, of course, even if you know everything about her."

"Which obviously I do not."

"She has worked hard to take charge of her life. In doing so, sometimes she does not realize how...hmm..."

"Imperious?" Cahill tried.

"That's rather strong, but it's in the right category. But there's something else, and it stems from the abusive relationship with her pastfather. He never missed an opportunity to tell her how wrong she was. She did not tell me this in so many words. I was able to assemble a partial view of the abuse she suffered, both by his hands and by his...mouth."

Cahill considered. "So telling her she is wrong about something is what triggers her."

"*Précisement, mon ami.*"

"And I just gave her one big trigger."

"She'll get over it. Try to be there when she does."

"Yeah. Try. All right, what's the damage?"

"That depends on the method of payment," Margle reminded him.

"Yes, of course. I was thinking cash. Crisp, unreportable banknotes."

"*Tu es un vrai ami!* One thousand thalers even. That will cover the next two days of observation as well."

Cahill paid up. "Visiting hours?" he asked.

"For you, whenever you show up. There's always a receptionist at the front desk. And Recovery Room 3 has a very comfortable bed. Nohana should be awake around time for supper." He slid from the desk. "*Talley's Tavern* three doors down is known for its... ah, liquid cuisine."

Now what, thought Cahill, sitting alone in a booth and working on his second and last ale. Ayvy had left him and Nohana without transportation. Would she come back in a day or two? He had no read on her. A moment later he tokked his Palmetto for Pallas, the 'skipcomp for his *Akila*, and remoted the craft to the docksite behind Margle's clinic. This solved at least one problem with hardly any effort at all. He doubted other resolutions would arrive so easily.

Cahill started to take a sip, only to be greeted by the bottom of the mug. Not yet finished pondering, he weakened his resolve and signaled for one more ale. A tiny voice tickled his ear hair with a caution that such weakness had led to five years of seclusion. He gave the voice a peremptory nod, and used the fresh mug to froth himself a mustache.

What, he thought, about Nohana?

Thoughts roiled like gray cumulus, a hodge-podge of worries and concerns. On her own, he expected, she would do all right, especially if he bought her a spaceskip. But the very notion of that meant separation, division... solitude for both of them.

A sip and a gulp.

But could they remain together. The truth was that he loved Nohana. The truth was that she loved him. But it amounted to only two-thirds the love in the Unit.

A gulp.

And there was her age. No longer did that fret him. His acceptance of her as her was total. But...

Oh, goddesses, but. She was half his age. He had already seen signs on Forest Fens that others regarded her as his daughter, an observation of which he and Ayvy had not disabused them. He did not fear the snide remarks, but could he in good conscience allow them to reach her ears as well?

A gulp. And another.

To keep her, or to let her go. To be, or not to be.

A trickle. Autonomically he ordered another. Halfway through it, he came to a realization that truly disturbed him: he was deciding for her. But the future, together or individual, was her decision as well.

A shadow loomed over him, attired in a disheveled white apron. "If you'll forgive me, Mac," said the bartender, "I think you should make this your last one."

"Liquid cuisine," mumbled Cahill.

He paid the tab, and wobbled back to the clinic.

"You need some solid food," Nohana said.

She was sitting up erect on the bed, her back touching nothing and a thick soft pad under her rump. The expression on her face was one of love and pity.

"Or some strong coffee," he said.

She shook her head. "I've found that when you give coffee to a drunk, you don't get sobriety, you get a wide-awake drunk."

"I'm not drunk."

She tilted her head at him, and grinned.

"Can I go with tipsy?" he asked.

"This time, yeah." Her face saddened. "Pol, what's happened?"

He sat down on the bed beside her and told her, including Margle's explanation, and omitting nothing but his own ruminations in *Talley's Tavern*.

"She still has not come to grips with her past," said Nohana, when he had finished. For a few moments she leaned her head on his shoulder—comfort food for the starving. She broke the silence with a quiet prod. "There's more, isn't there?"

He told her of his ruminations, and of his questions regarding the viability of their relationship. With each word, her expression grew fonder.

"'Whither thou goest, there will I follow,'" she said to him. "'Thy people shall be my people, and thy God my God.' Naomi, to Ruth, Pol. Do you know that one?"

"I've heard it," he allowed.

"I'm Naomi, Pol. That is my vote in this decision. I love you. I'm staying." She paused, the moment lambent now. "What do you want, Pol?"

"You." This without hesitation.

"I'll have to be on top for a while. My back, you know."

Despite himself, he laughed. In the wake of her lightheartedness his worries faded in intensity to nothing at all. Almost nothing. There remained one other point to resolve.

The resolution came from Nohana even before he broached the matter.

"One of two things must be true," she said. "Either she will return in the next two days, hopefully to work things out, or she will not return. In the latter instance... Pol, we go look for her. She's a 'whither-thou-goest' person, too."

And it was settled.

In the middle of the night in Recovery Room 3, Cahill awoke, and struggled to return to sleep. His position on the pad shifted every five or ten seconds. At one point, he kicked the hospital quilt completely off the bed...

...only to have it laid back over his body.

Blinking, he sought shapes in the utter darkness. A faint and pungent scent of antiseptic reached his nostrils. He was on the verge of identifying the source when she rested her hand on his bare chest.

"Nohana," he breathed.

"I had a bad dream." She sat down on the edge of the bed. "I dreamt you were falling, and I couldn't," he heard her swallow hard, "I couldn't catch you."

"I'm right here, Nohana."

"I know. That's why I came in. Pol." She turned to him. "Will you hold me tonight?"

"You never have to ask, Nohana."

By the end of the second day, Ayvy had yet to return, and Margle cleared Nohana from observation. Gingerly she walked alongside Cahill to the *Akila* docked out back. Once aboard, they sat in the captain's chairs on the bridge—he provided her with the additional cushion of a pillow from the stateroom—and gazed out the Videx at the local landscape of Gingham Dog.

It was pointless to check Pallas for messages, for they would have arrived on Cahill's Palmetto as well. Still, the request gave him something to do, in a moment when he needed to do something, anything.

"Pallas, any messages?"

"No. I'm sorry, Pol."

"Scan the Confederation for any mention of Angrboda Vigdisdottir over the past three days," he instructed, and held his breath.

"There are only reports that Confederation Security is still looking for her. And for you, Pol, by name. And for...a girl. Shall I set course somewhere?"

His lips puffed out with his sigh. Whether it was of relief or anxiety, he did not know. "Pallas, wait one," he said, and turned to Nohana. "What do you suggest."

For a long moment she considered, and he did not interrupt. At last she said, "If I had a bitter spat with my lover, and we fell out, I think...I think until I could pull myself together, I would go home."

"Pallas, set course for Tritonia and enTrack."

003: Distractions

Ayvy's arm flopped out on the sleeping pad, reminding her once again that, aside from herself, the stateroom bed and her life were empty. Fully awake now, she lowered her feet to the deck and sat up. Fingertips liberated sleep sand from her eyes. She felt no disorientation, for she knew very well where she was: in null-space, on a false-flag spacecraft, with a realtime location near her home world of Tritonia.

Once again she wondered what she was doing. And what she was doing *here*.

Her mother lived on Tritonia. Vigdis Olafsdottir. Daughter of Colin McKey, a name changed from Olaf Mikkelsson—her pastfather. Despite his persistent nagging, she had never changed her own name to suit him. Her declaration of independence. Ayvy wished she, too, had had the strength early on to oppose him. But she was, had been, a child. Was that an excuse?

Still she sat, awake. You have to do something, she told herself. Sleep, downdock, go elsewhere. Do *something*. You can't just sit here in null-space.

"Why not?" she muttered at herself.

If only Nohana were here...

Nohana. Pol. Doing something good with her life.

She felt herself weeping, for no reason at all. Angered by the tears, she pressed them away with fierce sweeps of the palms of her hands. Weeping did not become her. Her pastfather had told her that.

Damn him...

A weary sigh followed. She tokked her Palmetto for her mother. She needed the comfort of a familiar voice, the touch of a familiar hand on her head, her cheek, the side of her neck. But no response issued from her device. What did that mean? The Palmetto was an integral part of life. Unlikely that her mother had left it behind while out shopping, or engaged in the hygiene alcove.

Mom?

Panic hovered within her, and she batted it away like a pesky insect. For her, Tritonia was a danger zone. She needed a clear head to consider all aspects of visiting the surface. She was wanted by the security authorities. Almost certainly she was being sought by her pastfather's associates. Worse, if he had failed to change his will, she had inherited his properties and his estate, the wealth and control of which was sure to be disputed by the very-safe. If they could lock her away forever, or kill her outright, they could divide the spoils with impunity. When she had rifled his caches of money, she had only confiscated a small portion of his liquid assets. The very-safe would want even that returned to them.

Yet she had to dock down in order to reach her mother.

Forestalling what she knew to be inevitable, she tokked her Palmetto again, with the same result.

There was no choice. Not now.

Ayvy downdocked at the Hamillon Spaceport under the name Virginie LaCroix, captain and owner of the spaceskip *Garnet Sky*, the false-flag identity and transponder installed by Cahill along with several identities. To match the description that went with LaCroix, Ayvy cut her hair back to the nape of her neck, and dyed it jet black, and fitted pearl-gray lenses to her eyes. Small wads of cotton between her cheek and upper teeth altered the configuration of her face, as did an injection of saline solution just above each eyebrow and at the point of her jaw. It was not a change sufficient to foil facial recognition software completely, but it would slow it down and give her time to get away.

Attired now in a royal blue outsuit, she left the 'skip in a private hangar and went to the Spaceport admin office to arrange the let of an airfoil. Staying in character, she insisted on a deep blue one with black detailing that went with her outsuit and hair. Should the clerk ask, he would remember her; should he be shown a flat-print likeness of Ayvy, he would have denied knowing her. It wasn't much of an advantage, she thought, as she climbed aboard and powered up. But when you've nothing to lose, you have to call your own shots.

A frontal approach to her mother's cottage was out of the question until she put in some recon. On the way to that neighborhood, she raised Freya on her Palmetto.

"Freya, realtime scan of the area around my mother's house," she instructed. "You're looking for anything suspicious—"

"Oh how would I know what looks suspicious?"

"Freya," Ayvy said patiently. "Look for people lurking about, or watching the house. They might even be smelling the flowers—"

"Smelling flowers constitutes suspicious activity?"

"Freya," she sighed. Gathering herself, she went on, "Do you remember when I made lefse, and I put a wrap of still-warm lefse on the instrumentation console for your sensors to detect and analyze?"

"Oh, how I love that smell!"

"Yeah. If you ever want me to do that again, you'd better check out the area around that cottage. Look for people, drones, mechanical objects, electromagnetic emissions, anything that might indicate the cottage is being watched. *Skilur þú mig?*"

Sounding sullen, Freya replied, *"Ég skil."* Then, with grave seriousness, *"Ég skil, Angrboda. I am scanning now."*

"Takk fyrir. I'll pick up some potatoes and heavy cream if I find a store."

"The flour in the galley is old."

"I'll put it on the list."

"I detect nothing physical in the area. However, the null-space electromagnetic spectrum is being monitored for incoming communications."

Ayvy swore. "I should have thought of that before I tried to raise Mom. Well, as there is a false origin from my Palmetto, whoever is listening in will wonder why *Foley's B&G* on Margent is trying to raise her. All right, thank you, Freya. Continue scanning."

The glideways became narrower and more intricate as Ayvy skirted the center of Hamillon and made for the suburbs in the northern part of the city. There she found the parks she remembered, and the tables and the little rodents who scavenged on leavings from picnickers, and the swings. Some years had passed since last she had seen these, and she soon discovered that even these simple places and things brought a few tears of nostalgia to her eyes. But this reminiscence was soon replaced by her memory of the man who had destroyed her childhood. Who had told her what she would be and what she would do, in no uncertain terms. Whom she had shot dead not so long ago, her final response to his demands and to his abusive ways.

Ayvy shook her head clear of bad memories. Drawing onto the glideway that led to her mother's cottage, she felt her heart soar. There had always been a hug and freshly-baked bread for her in that house, and rooms with no shouting. Quiet places where she could gather her thoughts. In the back yard grew a tree, something native but like an oak, branches spread like a mind open to all possibilities. Like Nohana was.

Damn it, she seethed, at the unbidden name. Nohana had everything Ayvy wished she could have had.

So why are you standing in the way of her growth?

Ayvy blinked. Such unwanted thoughts stabbed at her now and then, and she had no way to beat them back into submission. Nohana and she were...were...

Sisters. Companions. Lovers. Partners.
Kindred spirits.
And you gave her up. You gave Pol up.

"Stop!" Ayvy yelled at herself, and almost lost control of the airfoil. Children playing in a yard paused to gape at her, a ball falling to the grass at their feet.

She looked ahead. There was the cottage. Her refuge; her safe haven. Purple flowers on either side of the front steps. Flowers in shades of gold around the perimeter of the front yard. The veranda still needed a new support post for the roof, and the deck could stand repainting. This time, this visit, she would see to the repairs. She brought the airfoil to dock in the open spot to the side of the front yard, and climbed down.

Hastened to the front door. Only the screen door was closed; the front was open. She sniffed the air, hoping for a scent of bread, or perhaps cookies. Without knocking, she stepped into the front room.

From the sofa in the front room rose three men. The one in the middle said, "Angrboda Vigdisdottir, you are hereby detained for the murder of Colin McKey. Stand where you are and be shackled."

004: Holmes & Watson

The Track from Gingham Dog to Tritonia covered almost three hours. After he briefed Nohana on what to expect of that world, they moved aft to the staterooms to get some rest. Cahill was puzzled when she followed him into his stateroom.

"Nohana?" he said, with unspoken questions on his face.

All her incisors gleamed at him in the overhead light. "Not that I would mind that," she said, and grew solemn. "I think it's separation anxiety. I don't want to be alone. But if you...you want me to leave, I-I will."

"I didn't plan the berths in the two staterooms for double occupancy," he said, with a glance at the sleeping pad.

Her hands against his chest eased him back toward the berth. "That's an easy solve," she told him.

Cahill did not know how long he had dozed, and he did not want to awaken Nohana by asking Pallas. The 'skipcomp had not yet announced arrival, so he estimated two hours. Not that it mattered. He had gotten the rest he needed, and Nohana was still gathering hers. Her eyelids fluttered, and he wondered what she was dreaming. Hopefully it was not another nightmare of him falling.

Gently he shifted so that a little space separated their upper bodies. He propped himself up on his left elbow and watched her sleeping. She lay on her right side, her hand and forearm under the pillow that cushioned her cheek. For a moment he reached out with his right hand, intending to touch the backs of his fingers to her cheek. But he drew back lest he complete the caress and awaken her.

In that moment, to his surprise, he found he wanted Ayvy there instead of Nohana. Not for intimacies, and not as a matter of preference. But Ayvy, despite her many fine qualities, was a broken, tarnished doll. He wanted to repair her, and make her shine. No, that was not quite correct. He wanted to help her repair herself, so that she shone.

He missed her.

"Are we there yet?" asked Nohana, blinking.

The sound of her voice brought him back to the reality of her.

She yawned, and stretched. "You see, I was right. There is enough room for two."

"Only because we removed our footgear."

She put a finger to her cheek, thinking. "So the more clothing we take off, the more room we'll have in bed."

Cahill sighed. "And on that note, I think I'd better get up."

"I think you already are."

He swung his feet to the deck and sat up. "I have got to learn not to feed you straight lines. Go on, shoo. Take your boots with you. I'll meet you on the bridge. Coffee, or ginger ale?"

"Ginger ale," she said, and padded out the doorway.

Alone, Cahill felt a smile curl the corners of his mouth. Two months had passed, and yet Nohana still took some getting used-to. When necessary, she could be deadly serious, as she was when she rescued the infant. In other moments, she was as light as a cloud in a breeze.

When he reached the bridge, she said, "There's a message from someone named Zykier. Pallas was going to tell you when you got here."

He handed her a mug, put his own in the well on the console, and sat down. "What does he say?"

"I didn't ask. I didn't know whether I should listen to it."

"I asked him to check on something for me," Cahill explained. "Pallas, play message, if you please."

Though the voice was gruff, the tone itself was pleasant enough. "Pedar Zykier here, Pol. Two days ago you asked me to keep a quiet eye on Vigdis Olafsdottir, and I've done that. Nothing came up until now. But I don't know if it's what you want. Security is still looking for her. But the...McKey's associates in the corporations are not. They've stopped. But I don't know what it means. Hope it helps, and I'll keep that eye out."

"Message ends," said Pallas.

"That's bad, isn't it?" asked Nohana.

Cahill just looked at her.

"Okay, it's bad. How bad is it?"

"I suppose there are other interpretations," he said, unhappy. "But I think she has been taken prisoner by McKey's very-safe associates."

"But why? She hasn't done anything."

Cahill looked away. How to break it to her that this was closer to reality than life on Cullen's Lode? Nohana had ideals. But she needed to know about corporate society in general, in order to protect herself.

"What does 'very-safe' mean?" she asked.

"It refers to people who are so wealthy and/or so well-connected that they are able to do whatever they wish with impunity," he told her, unable to mask the disgust in his tone. "They even break their own laws while they prosecute you and me for breaking them. There have always been the very-safe, Nohana."

She shook her head. "Not on Cullen's Lode."

"No, I suppose not there. To answer your question: they are using Ayvy's mother to force Ayvy to come to them. They will torture Vigdis Olafsdottir to get what they want from Ayvy. But I don't know for certain what it is they want. Money, I suppose."

"If her pastfather was a very-safe, much of his wealth might be tied up in holdings, like the distilleries, which Ayvy might have inherited."

"I don't think she wants them," said Cahill. "She was trying to escape from that sort of future."

"But they wouldn't know that," Nohana pointed out. Briefly she considered. "Would Ayvy have come to Tritonia?" she asked.

Cahill shrugged. "This was your suggestion. It happens that I agree with it," he added quickly, before she could protest.

"*Tritonia,*" announced Pallas, and the world appeared in the Videx.

***

With the *Akila* false-flagged as the *Bagheera*, they downdocked under aliases, Paul Kipling and his niece, Ioanna Kipling. Like Ayvy before them, they let an airfoil and made for the suburb where Vigdis Olafsdottir lived. Unlike Ayvy, they set their airfoil two spots further up the glideway, and acted as if they were more interested in the cottage with the for-sale sign in the yard. Cahill's attire—expensive black slacks and a white shirt whose collar was bound by a modest blue cravatte—lent credence to their identity and purpose. From there, it was only natural that they check the neighborhood, listening for uncomfortable noises, and noting the upkeep of the front yards. Such an appearance was credible, but in order to actually approach the Olafsdottir home without arousing suspicion, Cahill had hit upon a time-honored procedure.

Accordingly, he and Nohana, who was primly attired in a white button-down blouse and brown slacks, with her hair bound in a bun, crossed the glideway and headed toward the first house at which someone was obviously at home. The woman, who appeared to be middle-aged at ninety or so, was trimming shrubbery in her front yard when they walked up to her.

With Nohana at a respectful one-pace behind and to the side of Cahill, he said, "Good morning, Madame," and handed her a business card. "We're from the Church of Latter Day Saints, and we'd like to talk with you about our Heavenly Father—"

"That's quite all right," said the woman. But she returned the card and went back into her cottage.

"A little rude," was Nohana's quiet assessment, as they headed for the next cottage. "Have you done this before?"

"I've used similar ruses when I worked for Confederation Security," he replied. "But not exactly like this, no." He took in their surroundings without appearing to do so, and lowered his voice. "I don't see anything suspicious."

At the next cottage, Nohana knocked, and presently a young man in his twenties came to the door. In one hand he carelessly held a bottle of beer. "Yeah?"

"Good morning, *M'sieur*," said Cahill. "We're from the Church of the Latter—"

"I don't do church," he said, and slammed the door in their faces.

"That was *a lot* rude," said Nohana, as they retreated.

"It's all part of the presentation," he told her. "Here we go."

The golden flowers in Olafsdottir's front yard looked stressed, as if they had not been watered that morning. On the way to the door, Nohana said, "It's just ajar."

"Yeah."

"Should I still knock?"

"For a ruse to work, you have to stay in character at all times."

Nohana grimaced. "I suppose there will be a quiz," she said, as she knocked. The blow moved the door in a few centimeters.

"True and false," said Cahill, again looking around inconspicuously. "A few multiple choice." He held out a card. "Ah, good morning, Madame. We're from the Church of Latter Day Saints, and we'd like to talk with you about our Heavenly Father…you would? That's wonderful. May we come in?"

He nudged the door open further, and they stepped inside. "Leave it open," he told Nohana.

"Still in character?"

"*Précisement*. But don't touch anything you don't have to."

The front room was simple, almost spartan, in layout. One sofa, with an end table of dark wood; a writing desk whose utility now included a potted plant; a set of shelving that contained oddments along the side wall, and a curtained window above it; a wine carpet, with a paler trapezoid faded by sunlight through the front window.

They put off a search until after they had checked the rooms for occupants. Having determined they were alone in the cottage, they returned to the front room.

"What are we looking for?" asked Nohana.

He shook his head. "I don't know. Anything that doesn't quite fit. I just want to get a feel for the place."

"How about a bit of ash?" she asked, standing now at the far end of the sofa.

Cahill stepped to her. "Where?"

She pointed to a spot on the carpet just in front of the sofa leg. Hands on knees, he bent down to examine it more closely. "Cheroot, I think," he said, and sniffed the air.

"Yeah," said Nohana. "It smells very faintly of flowers. Jasmine? Lilacs?"

"Something sweet," Cahill agreed, straightening. "They probably used an air freshener to cover the smoke."

She arched a brown eyebrow. "They?"

"She was abducted, Ioanna. Check the hygiene alcove and the bedroom closet. You're looking for signs they might have packed for her. Hygiene items, clothing. I want to get a look at the back yard."

The yard consisted of stepping-stone paths that wound past clusters of flowers and shrubs, as if the occupant took a slow daily walk in appreciation of nature in this yard. Cahill counted but two trees, possibly as old as Ayvy's mother, both abound with broad leaves this time of year. Neither appeared to be fruit-bearing.

But there was an area on the walkway where several of the stones appeared to have been displaced, as if by a docked craft.

"Found something," Nohana called.

He strode toward the sound of her voice, and found her in the bedroom. She was standing before an open closet door. "What is it?"

"Nothing."

His brow bunched. "Ioanna?"

"Look in the closet."

He did so. "I don't see it."

"As you said, *précisement*. There is nothing wrong in this closet. There are seven empty hangers on the rod against the left wall. There are no other empty hangers. Neither she nor anyone else packed clothing for her, at least not from this closet. There's nothing missing. No unexplained empty hangers."

"Maybe they took the hangers, too."

She nodded. "Yeah, but that would mean they were taking her to a place where she could hang them up. That's inconsistent with abduction or detention." She turned and headed out of the bedroom. "But there's more."

"More nothing?"

She laughed. "In a way," she said, and led him into the bathroom. There she pointed at several toiletries. "Power toothbrush, dental paste, floss, bottle of mouthwash, depilatory cream, body lotion. It's all there. But it gets even worse." She picked up a bottle of pills and handed it to him. "Warmodden," she said. "Blood thinner. She may have had a clotting problem. Or too much clofibrate in her system. I don't know; I can't tell from that. But when you don't take your blood thinner, you run the risk of clotting, which can cause strokes, heart stoppage, and phlebitis, among other problems."

"That was quite a school you attended on Cullen's Lode," he said, returning the bottle to her.

She shook her head. "Some of that is on the label," she said. "The rest is a simple matter of reasoning it out." Her eyes narrowed at his reflection in the mirror above the sink. "You see the implications."

"She was abducted," he said. "And they do not expect to return her."

"Yeah," she sighed.

Her right canines worried at the lining in her cheek as she stared vacantly through the mirror. Her thought process was almost palpable, and Cahill wondered what was going through her mind. They had seen the same things, but she had different filters for analyzing what she had seen.

"Something?" he said at last.

Nohana turned away from the mirror. Her expression said she could not quite put her finger on what was wrong. "Paul...you've had experience with security matters. Would you say the abduction was a professional job? Because I don't know how to evaluate it."

Briefly he considered. "Aside from a very small bit of almost-unnoticeable cheroot ash, and a few slightly displaced stepping stones in the garden, there's nothing to indicate foul play. So yeah, I'd say whoever took Vigdis Olafsdottir knew what they were about."

Frustration twisted her face. "But that's what's bothering me about all this," she said, as they headed back to the front room. "It's Vigdis Olafsdottir. She's probably in her early fifties, a couple decades to middle-age. She bakes bread. She lives alone, as far as we can tell. She tends a garden. I don't mean any disrespect to her, but she's hardly a danger to anyone. Surely she doesn't warrant a professional abduction effort. A couple of lowly minions could get the job done, and for a lot less money, I should think."

Already Cahill could see where she was going with this. He spat a few words that Nohana had heard down on the fishing dock on Cullen's Lode.

"They already had Vigdis," he said bitterly. He made fists, but there was nothing to strike out at. "They might have taken her when she went shopping. They sent the pros for *Ayvy*. They knew she would show up here."

"So they have both of them now," said Nohana, her tone dulled.

"They have both. And you know what that means."

"Torture?"

He shook his head. "Ayvy won't wait for that," he said. "She'll cave at the first move toward her mother. But that's not the worst of it."

Her eyes widened. "There's a worse?"

"When they're done with Ayvy and her mother, they'll kill them. They'll have to. Ayvy can cause too much trouble, and Vigdis is a witness."

"Oh, goddesses..."

He peered through the open front door. "We need to get out of here, now," he said, and took her hand.

"But what are we going to do?"

"We'll meet with Zykier. He knows the lay of the land, so to speak. Whatever we can do, it starts there."

005: Stone Walls a Prison Make

The cold hard floor chilled Ayvy into awakening. It also cleared her mind of the drug they had given her. Hooded, her arms and legs bound, she thought she lay on paving stones. Their edges were rough, abrasive; in between was some sort of mortar, now crumbling—which explained the grit on the stones.

Struggling, she finally gained a sitting position, which chilled only her butt and the soles of her feet. She debated trying to stand, and decided against it; falling on a floor of stone risked injury, and for no good reason. Instead, she considered her location. Chill air, cold stone. Soundless, save for her breathing and heartbeat. Vision would help. She began to focus on a means of removing the hood.

Made of opaque black cloth, the hood fit loosely over her head. If she could reach it with her hands, she might yank it off with ease. But her hands were bound behind her back. She needed something to grip the fabric. Presently she tilted her head inside the hood and bit the fabric, tugging it down, pulling it over her head. Centimeter by centimeter, this was working. The idle thought occurred to her that her captors were more concerned with what she might do with her hands and feet than with what she might see. As dim light from a single overhead panel flooded her face, she saw how that thought might bode ill.

As immediate recognition came to her, Ayvy looked around. She was in a cell of stone blocks, about three meters on a side and two meters high, with a wide opening that gave onto a corridor. There was no cell door, nothing to prevent her from leaving the cell. Except possibly an armed guard in the corridor. But where, exactly, was she?

Flexibility proved to be her next form of defense. She tested the slackness with which her hands had been bound behind her, and found that while the hands themselves were tight, there was considerable play between the bindings and her rump. Curling into a ball, she fought to bring her hands under her and around her bent legs. Her boots posed an obstacle to this action. Grunting and groaning, she finally managed to clear her bootheels and bring her hands up over the boots and in front of her.

Although she was still unable to free her hands, she dug her fingers into the knot at her ankles, and presently liberated her feet. She could now walk. But walk where?

Had her captors taken into account the possibility that she might free herself, at least to some extent? Were they waiting for her to do just that? Shot while attempting to escape?

Gaining her feet, she walked around the cell looking for an edge of stone that might serve to abrade the rope that bound her. The only one that looked suitable would also abrade her wrists, but that couldn't be helped. Five minutes and several thin trickles of blood later, she had freed herself.

Step to the opening. Peer around one corner, prepared to draw back at the first sight of anything at all. Nothing so far. Check around the other corner. Nothing so far.

Go big or don't go at all.

A deep breath fortified Ayvy. She stepped out into the corridor. It was illuminated by a series of openings that two millennia ago might have been firing points. Daylight stretched from each opening across the floor to the other wall, striping the corridor in shadow and light. At one end there was a turn to the right; at the other, twenty meters away, a heavy wooden door awaited her.

There did not appear to be any opening through which she might get a glimpse of what lay beyond the door, so she opted for the turn in the corridor. Having made that decision, she hastened, to help against the possibility that someone might come through the door. When she reached the corner, caution returned. She started to look around it, and jerked her head back, heart pounding.

A uniformed and armed guard was standing with his back to the wall, not three steps away.

***

"I feel lost," said Nohana.

They were sitting at an outdoor table off to one side, where there was scant chance of behind overheard. The table—round, metal, and painted gray, and with matching chairs—stood on the patio of the *Golden Crassus*, an upscale tavern on the east side of Hamillon. Cahill casually eyed the passers-by, scanning for a short, stocky, and swarthy man in his early forties—a configuration familiar to him from his ConSec days, for Pedar Zykier had been a useful, knowledgeable contact. Even in retirement, he kept his ear to the ground; one never knew which bit of information might prove critical in an operation.

The trace of a smile creased his lips. "We're right here," he said.

"Yeah. I think...for me, this is not a load of gold we're taking. The people we're opposing now are...are... they are unaccountable for their actions, Po...Paul. They're beyond all that. They frighten me."

"I never meant for you to receive a baptism of fire, Ioanna."

"I know," she said, reaching for his arm. "I know. It's all right. I take my cues from you, and keep my Singer pack fully charged." She sobered a little. "I hope she's all right."

A serving girl approached to check on them. "More coffee," she asked. "Something light to eat?"

She was about Nohana's age, but with yellow hair cut short to the bottom of her neck. A white apron covered her candy-stripe uniform. The tip of a Palmetto stuck out of an apron pocket. Her name tag read Shimmer. Cahill was unable to avoid noticing the differences between her and Nohana. Their cultures and education were in no way even similar.

"Paul?" said Nohana.

"Ah...yes, some warm rolls and butter, please, and refills on the coffee," he said. "Ioanna?"

"That'll do me as well."

Shimmer departed. Nohana said, "We're not the same, Paul."

The statement took him aback. "Confederation Security has a job for you, reading people," he told her.

"Pass on that. I like where I am. The pay is terrible, but the side benefits are to die for. Paul… everyone is different. There is nothing wrong with the job she does. She seems competent and amiable, which is what an employer wants. I know; I used to work in *The Blue Snooter*, remember? You can't judge a person by the position they hold, but by the way they go about their duties."

"More guidance?" he asked.

"Plus training on the job. I like her name, though."

His tone warned her. "He's here. Coming up on your right side."

She moved her chair a little to accommodate Zykier's approach. He sat down without invitation, his body thumping the chair and jostling the table. His eyes took in Nohana first, but he made no comment to her, and gave her but a nod of greeting.

"I wasn't followed," said Zykier, before Cahill could ask. "What names are you going by here?"

"Paul and Ioanna Kipling. Why would you be followed?"

"You and I are known associates," Zykier answered, as if that should have been obvious.

"Not for seven years—"

"That means nothing to these people. You don't know them, Paul."

"Acquaint us with them," growled Nohana.

***

As Ayvy stood by passively, her options now uncertain, she heard a faint tinny sound, immediately followed by a waft of smoke. The guard, perhaps thinking he was alone, had lit up. But what was he guarding?

Fight or flight? But flee where? And if she fought, and won, what then? She had one advantage: the guard was unaware of her. But that could change at any moment. She had to be proactive.

One more check on his location...

He spotted her!

Reacting instantly, she drove four knuckles into the nerve center just below his sternum. Gasping for breath, unable to cry out, he slumped against the wall. His cigarette dropped to the floor. Ayvy followed up the blow with a knee to the groin and a hand-blade to the back of the neck. He was unconscious even before he sprawled onto the floor.

Ayvy decided not to kill him. If she were to be recaptured, that mercy might work for her. The end of this corridor beckoned, for daylight shone directly at her now. She ran toward it, hoping for a way out. When she reached the window, vertigo struck her for a few seconds. The wall with the window stood atop a cliff. She could see forever in the distance. Far away and below spread the city of Hamillon. Her heart turned to lead as she realized where she was.

There was no way out, except the way she had been brought in. She was a prisoner within the Chateau de la Paix.

***

"This is how it works," said Zykier, after Shimmer brought him a mug of ale. He spoke mostly for Nohana's benefit; Cahill knew much of it, but also knew that there had been changes since last he was active.

"Local governments are elected to keep people in line," he went on. "Generally they are not oppressive, although they can be. But their powers and authority are nominal. They do what the corporate hierarchs tell them to do."

"I understand that," Nohana said stiffly.

"Yes. Well, every once in a while, something egregious occurs, and it becomes necessary to throw one of the hierarchs to the wolves, in a manner of speaking. That is the only way these people give up any of their power. Now, the question I have been asking is how all this relates to Colin McKey and his death. It's been called murder by the authorities, but from what I know of the investigation, it looks like self-defense. But even that is not important in this matter. Angrboda Vigdisdottir is the sole name that appears in McKey's will. She is his sole inheritor. The value of McKey's holdings and accounts is...almost beyond calculation. The Bank of Tritonia knows what he was worth, but they are not disclosing that, at least not publicly."

As Shimmer returned with the order of rolls and a coffee carafe, Zykier paused to drain half his ale and signal for another. After the serving girl departed, he went on, "Hierarchs can never have enough. Not power, not position, not property, not...what else begins with a p?"

"*Pecunia*," said Cahill, adding to Nohana, "Latin for 'money.'"

"Just so. At the moment, they are vultures picking over a carcass. But it has to be made legal, see? They can't just grab. They have to have permission to grab. And that's where Vigdisdottir comes in. She has to be made to surrender her inheritance. Her captors will use her mother to, ah, persuade her."

"Where are they holding her?" asked Cahill.

He grimaced. "Aye, there's the rub."

"*Hamlet*, Act III," said Nohana.

Zykier turned to her. "Who exactly are you again?"

"Someone who has read *Hamlet*. You were saying?"

For several seconds, Zykier held her steady gaze. "Yes, of course," he said, turning back to Cahill. As Shimmer returned with the next ale for Zykier, he spoke in a voice that chilled him. "She's being held in the Chateau de la Paix."

Air fled Cahill as he sat back.

006: The Light in the Tunnel

Even as Ayvy grasped her location and predicament, she heard the echoes of heavy footsteps in the corridor. She turned around to see, but nobody was there, yet. The guard she had fought still remained unconscious on the floor. She moved into the adjacent corridor and peered around the corner, waiting for the arrival of the footsteps. But they stopped too soon. She guessed the guards—or someone—had paused by her cell, only to find it empty. Next they would discover the guard on the floor. The search for her would then begin in earnest. She doubted it would be pleasant.

Cautiously Ayvy moved back to the window. The cliff wall dropped almost straight down a good hundred meters. Descent without rope for rappelling was impossible. To the right side, however, ran a ledge half a meter wide. She might walk it, but there were no handholds that she could see to help her with her balance. A gust of wind might well blow her off. Still, if she lay flat, she might hide out there while the guards searched the rest of the castle. And there was a metal drainpipe, of the sort that cleared waste from water closets at each level of the castle. It ran from the top level all the way down the wall to the cliff itself, and came to a stop where the detritus from the rock formed a slope she might slide down if she could reach it.

The pipe hardly seemed worth the effort. It looked old and rusted, and probably had not been used for a century or more. If it gave way while she descended...but she tried not to think about that. In any event, her mother might be held here as well, and Ayvy was unable to desert her.

What then?

Other cells along the corridor were open. She might wait in one of them. Perhaps the guards would pass hers by, unwilling to credit that she would hide in plain sight. At the very worst, they would take her to a cell with a door. She had to be kept alive until she did what they wanted...whatever that was.

Discretion the better part of prudence, to say nothing of valor, Ayvy selected a cell at random and entered it, sitting on the floor in a front corner where she might at least avoid a casual, careless glance.

***

"That's bad, isn't it?" asked Nohana.

"It was built almost three centuries ago by a hierarch who fancied living in a castle," said Zykier. "It could not function as a stone fortress, of course, or as a defensive redoubt, because it could be reduced to rubble by an artillery unit. But it pleased the hierarch to live there, with his servants and staff. He even developed a medieval torture chamber, complete with rack and iron maiden and heated tongs. It was said, but never proven, that he invited the impoverished into the castle for a meal, and once there, after feeding them, he took them into the dungeon, and no one ever saw them again." Nohana gasped, and he quickly added, "As I said, it was never proven. He was a recluse, and such individuals are usually the target of negative speculation, baseless though it might be."

"But do you think it was baseless?" Nohana asked, in all seriousness.

"After the hierarch died, ownership of the castle passed on to one who had a darker outlook. A despot who ruled the township of Hamillon, as it was then, he did what his predecessor had been rumored to do, and more. It was during this time that the castle gained its name, the Castle of Peace, quite the opposite of the activities within. He and his descendants ruled for more than a century with an iron fist. But, like all things, they passed away, and the Chateau de la Paix became a museum of sorts. But access to the lower levels remained open only to those few who knew how to get in there, and how to bypass or suborn the guards. Again, negative speculation prevailed. Sometimes it was more than accurate; other times, there was nothing to it."

"But Ayvy is being kept there," said Cahill. "How do we get her and her mother out of there?"

Zykier shrugged. "I don't think you do."

"That's not good enough," snapped Nohana.

"It's as good as it gets, young woman." To Cahill, he said, "If you decide to try a rescue—which I do not recommend—and you need some equipment, I may be able to arrange it for you. But I..." He shook his head, and stood up. "It's up to you. Thanks for the ale," he finished, and turned to merge with the passers-by.

While Zykier passed from sight, Nohana toyed with her drink. "He wasn't much help."

"He didn't come here to help," replied Cahill. "He came to inform. Depending on what we decide to do, he'll handle what logistics he can."

"What *are* we going to do?"

"We're going to get Ayvy and her mother out of there and away from here," he said.

"Just so that's clear."

"But I don't know how we're going to do it."

Her eyes searched his. "Yet," she said.

"I love your confidence."

The overhead sun now began to nod off toward the southwest. Neither Cahill nor Nohana had anything to say until the serving girl arrived, and delicately cleared her throat for attention.

"I'm getting off my shift now," she said, despite her smile the hint heavy behind her words.

"Yes, of course," said Cahill, and passed her a hundred-thaler note, waving off the substantial change as a gratuity.

Shimmer folded the banknote and stuck it in her apron pocket. She started to turn, and changed her mind. "I'm sorry," she said. "I don't mean to eavesdrop. But I... your friend mentioned the Chateau de la Paix. Are you planning to take a tour there?"

Cahill's voice faltered momentarily; Nohana retained hers. "Why do you ask?"

"Oh. Well, before I came here, I used to work there," Shimmer replied. "I was a tour guide."

44

Nohana pulled a chair back. "Have a seat."

"Let me go clear my bills, first. I'll be right back."

As Shimmer dashed off, Nohana and Cahill exchanged glances.

"Maybe," he said. "Just maybe. But we have to be cautious in how we proceed, and how much we tell her."

"Why?"

He looked at her as if she had just uttered a phrase in a language he did not understand.

"If it's a matter of trust," Nohana went on, "consider that a few months ago I was doing the same sort of work she's doing now. I tended bar, I served customers, I solved the attendant problems as they arose. I did my job well. Patrons trusted my service."

"That's you," said Cahill.

"That's Shimmer as well," she shot back. "You have zero complaints about her job performance. You trust me to do my job. You can trust her. She is who she presents herself to be. If she's to help us in any way, she needs what facts we have."

"But she could—"

"She won't." For a moment she fell thoughtful. "I wouldn't talk out of turn," she went on. "Bartenders' code. Neither will Shimmer. We have to tell her." A meaningful look past his shoulder announced her return. "Let me do the talking," she finished.

Shimmer took the chair that had been offered her. In the interim, she had doffed the apron and the candy-stripe uniform, shagged her short yellow hair, and now was wearing a cropped yellow jersey and a pleated floral skirt that fell to a few centimeters above her knees, and comfortable gray loafers that matched her eyes.

"Laundry day today," she said, while Nohana inspected her.

"I like it," said Nohana. "I can just hear the witnesses talking to the security investigators." She lightened her voice. "That's right, officer. About a meter seventy-five, maybe I don't know, sixty kilos, smooth tan, nothing under the top, nice legs, you know?" Now her voice deepened, then reverted with the response. "But what about the two she was with? Oh, them? Some couple. Didn't really look at them, you know what I mean?"

Shimmer fell to laughter. "Who are you?" she managed.

"Someone who has done the same sort of work as you, Shimmer," Nohana told her. "I used to wear short skirts, until some man tried to put his hand...well, never mind."

"I've been there," said Shimmer.

"Yeah. Listen, is there someplace we can go? I think you've guessed by now that we have a little more than a tour in mind."

Cahill hissed at this, but made no remark.

Shimmer pointed to her right. "I live just a quad away," she said. "It's not much, but you're welcome."

007: Going Gently

The echoes of boots alerted Ayvy. She moved her empty hands into plain view and waited for the inevitable. Pauses in the echoes suggested they were searching each cell carefully. When a uniformed guard stepped into view in her cell, she got to her feet, raised her hands, and waited.

Though she was shoved roughly in the direction they wanted her to go, she was not otherwise abused. The guards did not even bind her hands. She concluded that her captors had wanted her to try to escape, so that she would learn the futility of it first-hand. But she was not returned to her original cell. Instead, she was placed on a lift and taken down five levels to the rooms well under the main part of the castle.

The lift doors opened to a darkness broken only by a rectangle of light that seeped past a doorway. One guard spoke a simple command, and the panels in the corridor ceiling began to glow. The corridor was empty, and the rooms had closed doors. She knew without asking that this was the level of the castle from which rumors escaped. But what was in that room to which they were leading her?

The door slid open at a touch to a wall panel. The interior was well-lit, and Ayvy blinked rapidly as she was led inside. White walls and ceiling reflected and amplified the light. Furnishings were spartan, and made the purpose of the room all too clear. A desk, and chairs behind and in front of it. The one behind had arms and a cushion, and appeared to be castered, as the man seated in it spun it around as she entered. The chair behind was of simple design, and all wood. Even had the man not been sitting, she would have known which chair was meant for her.

Ayvy recognized the man immediately. Had he been standing, she would have been a head taller. Why, she wondered, were all the evil people so short? The chair seemed too large for him; in her view, he needed a booster seat. His dark brown hair style came from a top-grade salon. She had no doubt his nails—fingers and toes—had been given the same attention. Even his outsuit looked bespoke, and not off the rack. But it was his face that forced her to suppress a smile. Despite his attempt to present a stern and dour look, the effort made his face a caricature of itself. It was as if Gandhi had learned German and was giving a speech at Nuremberg; it just wasn't working.

As the guards led her to the wooden chair, Ayvy looked around to be certain that she had not missed anything. Her mother was not present. Not yet, anyway.

The name of the man behind the desk was Varrell Thibodeaux, and his vineyards and wineries provided over ninety percent of the wines in the Confederation. Ever acquisitive, he had approached Colin McKey on several occasions regarding the sale of the McKey Distilleries. Ayvy had even been present at three of those meetings, where she had learned that greed actually had an odor around it, like a glob of vomit three days under the sun.

On top of the desk was a Palmetto, and nothing else. The device was sufficient to effect a legal transfer of property. As a guard shoved Ayvy down into the chair, she noted that the Palmetto was arranged so that she could read the screen. She had expected to see a document there. What she saw was the face of her mother.

***

Shimmer's apartment hardly warranted the term. Consisting of one room with a small dinette and a hygiene alcove, it was scarcely large enough to accommodate one occupant, much less three. The twin bed served as a sofa. The short counter that cordoned off the dinette served as a table for refreshments—in this case, green tea with honey-flavored syrup. As she sat down on the bed, Nohana wondered how much Shimmer was paid. But already the walls had gotten her undivided attention.

More than twenty paintings adorned the walls of the apartment. Most were done in oils or acrylics, a few in watercolors, and all in a style that clearly had been influenced by Impressionists like Monet and Morisot. Nohana saw landscapes of the imagination, reminiscent of the early Mitch Bentleys, worlds that existed only in the mind of the artist. None were framed, and hung only on canvas, as if the artist had only enough money for the materials but not the frames.

"You?" said Nohana.

Shimmer replied with a shy smile and a nod.

"You're *good*."

Cahill, in his ConSec mode, was inspecting the apartment itself with a critical eye when a sharp elbow in the ribs from Nohana compelled him to stop. After serving tea, Shimmer unfolded a metal chair and sat facing them. Nohana thought the tea tasted weak, but kept that assessment from her expression, giving instead a nod of approval.

She began with a falsehood by presenting their aliases. In response, Shimmer said, "It's not my real name. That's Loma Merrix. But a boy once told me I was lovely to look at, like a mirage. He said I shimmered. I decided I liked the name, if not the boy. Which is why I don't think those are your real names."

"They're close," said Cahill.

"Are you...wanted for anything? Like, you know, fugitives?"

"No," said Cahill.

"Yes," said Nohana. "But it's not relevant to the problem at hand." She then proceeded to explain the circumstances surrounding Ayvy and her mother.

"Oh, I heard about that," said Shimmer, after Nohana had finished. "Every once in a while he used to stop by for coffee. He never tipped, he was never satisfied with the service. The other girls and I just wrote him off as a bad job...although he did get one girl fired for muttering something." Her face twisted a little. "What's an imprecation?"

"Think of it as bad language," said Cahill.

"Well, that's what he called it." Shimmer gave a light laugh. "He didn't care for her imprecations. Knowing Tarla, she probably did it." She crossed her legs and tucked her skirt around them, and sat back. "Now, tell me how I can help."

"First," said Cahill, "tell us why you want to help."

For just a moment, disbelief crossed Shimmer's face. It faded with a smile that gently mocked the request. "You mean, instead of cleaning up the messes of certain customers, fending off the advances of certain others, washing dirty dishes, and generally picking up after?" she said sweetly. She rubbed the tip of her nose with an index finger. "Goddesses, how could I give up all that, even for a day?"

Nohana laughed. Cahill said, "But you do it so well."

"A job's worth doing, *M'sieur* Kipling," she said, as if that explained everything.

"This one could be dangerous," he said.

"I'll try to be careful."

Nohana's hand on his arm stopped his response. "To do what we want to do, we may have to take a tour," she said. "But we're more interested in places inside the castle where tourists don't go."

Shimmer nodded as if she had expected as much. "I know how to get in there," she said. "But I may not be able to get you out. As far as I know, nothing goes on down there, but still there are guards. We were told they were posted to prevent looting. I suppose there is a lucrative black market demand for iron maidens." Her eyes narrowed a little. "May I ask why?"

"A friend of ours has been taken there against her will," said Nohana. "We'd like to take her back against the will of her captors."

"Does this have anything to do with the McKey murder?"

Cahill winced at the word. "Probably," he said. "Does it matter?"

"Not at all. Count me in. That is, if you'll have me."

"Our friend is his grand-daughter," said Nohana. "She's been accused of his murder."

"Thank you for telling me," said Shimmer. "I wondered. But it changes nothing. I'm still in."

Nohana leaned back on stiff arms. "What do you recommend?"

"There's no time like the present," said Shimmer. "Let's go take a tour."

***

"Where is she?" demanded Ayvy, as pain knifed through her skull. The bright lights in the room were giving her a headache that her shouting enhanced.

Thibodeaux took his time responding, as if he were in no hurry. "She should be headed for what they used to call the rack room about now." His fingertips caressed the Palmetto screen. "It has an audio link to the room which you should find interesting. If you like, I can have the device put on a stand so that you can watch."

"What," grated Ayvy, biting back an epithetic urge, "do you want?"

"You're stalling for time," he replied. "I can't imagine why. You have none, and your mother has even less."

A groan filled the room, the sound of a human being under actual physical pressure. Gradually it reached a crescendo.

"Stop it, stop it," screamed Ayvy. "Stop. Please... oh, goddesses, stop hurting her."

Thibodeaux tapped the screen to activate communication. "That's enough for now," he ordered. "Give her two minutes to recover."

Ayvy's voice fought through a choked throat. "You haven't," she said brokenly, "told me...what...you want."

Thibodeaux nodded curtly, and a guard swatted her across the back of her head. The sting of the blow was as nothing compared to the fear for her mother.

"There is a price to be paid when you waste my time," Thibodeaux said evenly. "Now that you have paid it, I'll tell you. You will sign over your entire inheritance to me, signifying that you do this without duress. You will also return the funds you stole from McKey's accounts after you murdered him."

"I spent some," Ayvy mumbled.

"You will replace it."

She decided not to fight that. "And in return?" she asked.

"Oh, this is not a negotiation," he said. "I would have thought that obvious." To the Palmetto, he added, "I believe the two minutes have expired."

"No!" shrieked Ayvy, and leaped out of the chair, only to be smashed back into it by the guard. Dazed, she could only listen to her mother's screaming. In the back of her mind she was aware that she was losing it. All the experience and training she had known in the past few years now availed her nothing. Anguish weakened her. Helplessness made her shoulders and her spirit sag.

Her mother's screams ended abruptly.

"Oh, goddesses," Ayvy moaned.

"Your agreement can stop this," he said placidly, hands folded on top of the desk.

Ayvy gave a feeble nod. He tokked the Palmetto and nudged it closer, so that she could lean forward and read it. Through grief she was unable to read the words or to scroll carefully through the documents, nor did she care what they said. She plowed through them to the bottom. The guard handed her a stylus. She scribbled her name as if she were dealing with an itch, and left her thumbprint in the square provided in the template. Her signature was unimportant now.

Thibodeaux turned the Palmetto so that he could read it. Finally he nodded, mostly to himself. "Your mother will be our guest down here until tomorrow, when this clears probate. And it will clear, never fear. I've already paid the Notary to ensure that." He looked past her to the guard. "Have her mother placed in a cell with a door this time," he said. "See to it."

"She needs her medicine," said Ayvy, still weak. "Her blood thinner..."

"We'll arrange something," Thibodeaux said vaguely. He beckoned toward the doorway, and she heard two sets of footsteps approaching. "As for you, you're to be remanded to the custody of Tritonia Security and detained, to be charged with the murder of Colin McKey, your pastfather." He flashed a wicked grin. "I understand there is eyewitness testimony to the murder. Goodbye, *M'selle* McKey. I doubt our paths shall cross again."

One of the security escorts pulled Ayvy to her feet as she spoke. "It's Vigdisdottir, you piece of—"

A hard blow from the escort silenced her.

***

"And over here we have the dining room," said Elin, the tour guide, a young woman not much older than Shimmer. She recognized Shimmer immediately, having worked with her before. Her warm blue eyes wondered why Shimmer had come to take a tour she herself had guided scores of times, but the question gradually passed as her rote narrative came to the fore.

Her voice, however, began to fade in Nohana's ears. She and Cahill and Shimmer were bringing up the rear of the dozen or so people who had signed up, the easier to ditch the tour when the time came. That Elin recognized and knew Shimmer, and would notice her absence, was unavoidable; worse, it meant that the three of them might have to rush the rescue.

"And we're walking..."

"Almost there," whispered Shimmer. "Around the corner, past the hygiene alcove, and into the utility closet, one by one. Wait inside until we're all three there."

Cahill stopped. "You're not coming in there with us," he said. "It's too dangerous."

"But I have the schematic," she pointed out.

"It's a century old, at least. It probably won't be accurate."

Nohana hissed. "A century old is better than nothing. Let's go!"

Still muttering a protest, Cahill kept them close to the other tourists. Elin the tour guide had immersed herself in her lines, emerging only to respond to intermittent questions. She kept the group walking, around the corner, and to another turn, and that was when the trio made their move.

They barely fit in the utility closet, which was also cluttered with cleaning equipment and various sprays. Nohana stumbled into a broom that clattered against the wall. On voice command from Cahill the overhead panel began to glow, and they stopped colliding with equipment. Opposite the door they had entered was a door that Shimmer assured them led into the depths of the castle. But it was impossible to know what, exactly, awaited them on the other side. To make matters worse, the door opened to the outside, and its movement could be more easily noticed.

"Let me go," said Nohana. "If I'm caught, I was looking for the hygiene alcove, and made a wrong turn. The tour guide can verify that I was in the group. If it's clear, I'll rap on the door twice, then twice again."

"I don't like it," said Cahill.

She touched his arm. "Pol, I love you, but if someone is out there, they'll be far more suspicious of a man than of me."

"She has a point," Shimmer threw in.

"Leave your Singer with me," he said. "If they find that on you, they'll know something's amiss."

Without a word she handed it to him. "Kill the light," she said. After it faded out, she opened the door wide, as if she expected to find herself back with the tour. Stay in character, she reminded herself: a lesson from Cahill. Her heart thumped as she glanced one way, then closed the door to see the rest of the corridor. For the moment, she was alone there. But she had no idea where she was. Yellow walls of cut stone block, lit by ceiling panels, seemed to extend forever. Faint sounds reached her, not of footsteps but of voices. They were too muted by distance to leave an echo. They came from somewhere to the right. She knocked the agreed code on the door, and was joined in the corridor by Cahill and Shimmer. She pointed in the direction of the voices.

"That way, I think," she said.

***

Gambled, thought Ayvy, *and lost*. She was barely aware of the security escort now bracketing her on the way to the door. They had not yet confined her hands; she knew more than enough moves to put the two men out of action. But what would be the point? Escape from the castle was impossible. Her mother was as good as dead—Thibodeaux had intimated as much by his relative lack of concern for her medicine—and she herself would be set up for execution, for a trial was superfluous, the court already having been paid for its verdict.

Worst of all, I've lost the three people I love most.

Pol...Nohana...what would they say?

But she knew the answer to that. Inwardly Ayvy almost smiled. *They'd say, you're still alive, aren't you? So do something.*

What was that phrase from her Lit class? Do not go gently into...no, wait, it was gentle. Gentle into that good night. Who said that? Waxworth? No, a couple centuries before her. Who...?

The back of her head hurt. She couldn't think; she'd been hit hard by the guard, neither gentle nor gently. As soon as the security team had her out the door, her fate was sealed. No, that was not true. She had sealed her own fate when she had Palmed her mother.

But I had to come. They would have taken her anyway, and killed her.

But they're going to kill me, anyway, too.

The thought galvanized her. Totally focused now, she yanked herself free from the grasp of one escort, and pivoted to disable the other with a spin kick...only to find that he was already on the floor. Assuming he must have slipped, she turned to continue dealing with the first escort. Now his weapon was out, and being brought to bear on her.

"Kill her!" yelled Thibodeaux. "Don't let her get away!"

008: Iron Maiden

Shimmer checked her schematic, and pointed in the direction of the faint voices. "According to this, there are cells in this direction, as well as some chambers for... well, for torture," she said.

"I hear more than one voice," said Cahill. "And... that's a scream."

They began to run, ignoring the echoes of their footfalls. The scream grew louder, then ended abruptly. Cahill, in the lead, waved them to stop, and placed his index finger over his lips for quiet. Some twenty meters ahead was an open doorway. Voices emerged through it. A man's voice. Ayvy's voice, dulled and sullen. Nohana's heart broke as she clutched the Singer Sizzler.

"We have to locate her mother," she whispered.

Cahill spread his hands helplessly. Shimmer pointed to a side corridor and said, "I think the scream came from down there. There are a couple of rooms...rack room, it says here, and...and I don't even know what these other devices are for. One of the rooms appears to have been a conference room, where audiences were held." She frowned thoughtfully. "That should have been on the tour."

Nohana said, "They're probably holding her mother in one of those rooms. Pol, you go find her. Shimmer and I will see to Ayvy." Cahill turned to move off, and stopped at her, "Pol?" When he turned back to her, she added, "I don't think we have any use for prisoners. Unless you do."

"None whatsoever," he said, and padded silently toward the first of the rooms.

"Can you fight?" Nohana asked Shimmer, as they crept toward the open doorway.

"I don't have a weapon."

"Not what I asked."

"I-I don't know. I guess I can try."

The ambivalent response compelled Nohana to change her plan. "No, Shimmer. You go for Ayvy, and help her. You'll know which one she is. Get her out of the way. I'll take the others."

"Who are you?"

"I get that a lot," said Nohana. "Just try to stay out of my line of fire. Shh."

With the door already open, stealth was no longer needed when they arrived. Nohana simply shot the first man she saw. Ayvy hardly noticed her; she and the man beside her were struggling over a weapon. It fired, the blue beam just missing Shimmer, who let out a yelp. Nohana's quick glance at her confirmed that she had not been hit. She fired once more, and the second man went down.

"See to Ayvy," she told Shimmer, and dashed toward the desk and the man just now getting to his feet. A third beam from the Singer took out the onrushing guard. She then turned the weapon on the man at the desk.

"Who are you?" he snarled. "How did you get in here? *Guards!*"

Nohana gestured at the Palmetto on the desk. "Did she sign?" she asked him.

"You're too late."

Nohana fired a steady beam at the Palmetto. First it melted, then it blew up, showering the man with molten bits of plastic. Pain raised the pitch of his voice as he tried to brush the hot fragments from his skin and clothing. A nudge at her arm made her whirl, ready to fire again.

"Easy," said Shimmer.

She had Ayvy in tow, shaken and wobbly. A thin line of blood trickled from Ayvy's hair down her forehead and off the tip of her nose. Azure eyes dulled by pain and fear stared vacantly at Nohana, as if wondering how she had come to be there.

"It's me," Nohana said gently, and curled a reassuring arm around her.

Cahill arrived then, weapon in one hand sweeping the room, and an older woman at his arm. Her brown outsuit, soiled by gardening, was in disarray and torn in places. Her face was pale from her ordeal, but she had enough strength left to stagger toward her daughter. While the others stood aside, she and Ayvy embraced.

"I gave her the pills," said Cahill, though it was not clear whether Ayvy heard.

Movement caught Nohana's eye, and she looked toward the man. He was just withdrawing his hand from the desk. Seconds later, the wail of a siren permeated the castle.

"They'll close off all the exits," said Shimmer, a tremble in her voice.

The man pointed his finger at her. "I know you," he said. "You're that trollop who works at the *Candystripe Café*."

"And you're the slug who likes to feel up the serving girls," Shimmer shot back. "You were out of luck the day you tried me. You're out of luck again today."

He chose the last refuge of a rich and powerful scoundrel. "Do you know who I am?"

Ignoring him, Nohana held the Singer out to Ayvy. "It's your honor," she said, in a tone as martial as a bugle call.

Still clinging to her mother, Ayvy declined the offer. "It's your rescue."

She swung the Singer back around. "Wait," was the only word Thibodeaux uttered before the beam struck his groin. He fell screaming, clutching at himself. "That was for Shimmer," she told him, and fired another beam into the bridge of his nose. "And that's for Ayvy's mother. The Unit sends its regards."

"The guards will be here any moment now," said Ayvy, beginning to recover.

Cahill took the schematic from Shimmer. "Where's that conference room?" She showed him. "Fast as we can, let's get there," he said.

Ayvy looked a question at him; Nohana gave voice to it. "What?"

"Got an idea," was all he said as they dashed along the side corridor.

Shimmer stopped suddenly, and waved her arms. "Here," she cried. "In here."

After they swept into a conference room the size of an auditorium, Nohana closed and secured the door. Cahill ushered them all against the nearest wall, and dug out his Palmetto.

"I don't understand," said Shimmer.

"I think I do," said Ayvy. "Incidentally, who are you?"

Cahill drowned out Nohana's response. "Pallas, do you have my coordinates?"

"Down to the micron."

"Put the bow of the *Akila* three meters from my signal, and Fastrack," he said. To the others, he added, "Hold on, there's going to be a burst of—"

A blast of displaced air buffeted them as the *Akila* downdocked inside the conference room. Yellow dust and grains from the stone walls swirled in the air. As soon as the ramp was extruded, they surged aboard. When Cahill reached the bridge, he said, "Pallas, enTrack. No destination."

"We're gone."

"Wait," cried Shimmer. "I can't go with you. My paintings!"

Already null-space filled the Videx. Cahill's lips puffed out with his sigh as he leaned on the instrumentation console, braced on stiff arms. Biting his lip failed to help him think. Finally he said, "We can drop you off at the Spaceport. We won't be down for longer than it takes you to disembark."

"I know," said Shimmer. She tried to sound sympathetic, but her voice shook as she spoke. "I can make my way from there. I just wish..." A wan smile crossed her face as she looked at Nohana. "I just wish there could be more."

"I suppose my house is out of the question now," said Vigdis Olafsdottir.

"I'm afraid so," Ayvy told her. "As soon as security figures out what happened, that would be one of the first places they'll look for us."

"Pallas," said Cahill. "I want a quick downdock at the Hamillon Spaceport. We'll stay for one minute only. Afterwards, set a course for Cullen's Lode and enTrack."

"Acknowledged."

He turned to Shimmer. "You'd better go aft and get in position," he said. "I can't risk any more time."

Shimmer saddened further. "I understand."

"I'll take her aft," said Nohana, and clutched her elbow. "Come with me."

"We are down. Spaceport Control has questions."

"Pallas, ignore them," said Cahill. Mentally he counted toward thirty, pulling up two seconds short.

"They are persistent."

"Retract the ramp and enTrack," he ordered, and null-space dulled the view in the Videx. Turning to Vigdis, he said, "We're going to Cullen's Lode, out in the Fringes. It is a world where you will be left alone, to live as you wish."

"We'll have a home for you," Ayvy added. "With the flowers and shrubs that you love. You'll be safe there."

"As long as I never have to start over again," said Vigdis.

"Where's Nohana?" asked Cahill.

Ayvy shrugged. "Somewhere aft."

A lump in his throat, Cahill said, "Pallas, where is Nohana?"

"She is not aboard the Akila."

Cahill slumped into his captain's chair. Desolation set in; his mouth felt full of sand. "Oh, she didn't…"

009: Desperate Measures

Nohana and Shimmer hid in plain sight among the spaceskips and shuttles docked on the Spaceport tarmac. Gradually, as if they were in no hurry, they made their way to the office of *Bad Bobo's Conveyances* to let an airfoil. The clerk was a balding and paunchy affable man who seemed to laugh for no reason at all. His name tag read Bad Bobo. There were no other customers in the office, but it took Nohana a moment to realize he was actually speaking to both her and Shimmer.

"You're here to let an airfoil, am I right?" he said, laughing as he belabored the obvious.

Nohana took out her fundscard. She still retained the false identity Cahill had given her. When she tried to pass it to Bad Bobo, he declined it. "You're too young to pilot an airfoil, am I right?" He turned to Shimmer. "What about you?"

Nohana sighed. "She's flying, I'm paying," and thrust the card at him once more.

He relented. "I guess we can do it that way." He scrutinized Shimmer from head to toe and back again. "I'd say a yellow or blue one, am I right? To go with your outfit? There's one out on the lot now that's blue with yellow detailing."

"It sounds fine," said Shimmer, slightly bored. She glanced at Nohana, who nodded. "One day, then. We'll bring it back tomorrow."

"By noon." Despite his laugh, he sounded apologetic. "After that, there's an extra charge."

Nohana shrugged as she signed the digital chit.

"You'll be wanting collision insurance as well, am I right?"

"No," said Nohana. "We won't hit anything, and if someone hits us, either they'll have insurance, or they won't, in which case it's a matter for the local authorities to see that you are reimbursed, am I right?" She waved to him on their way out the door. "Thanks. See you tomorrow, before noon."

Moments later, with Shimmer at the helm, they were headed for her apartment. "I still don't understand why you did this," she said. "I mean, it's obvious that, despite your age, Paul is in love with you, and you didn't see the affection in that woman's eyes when you came to rescue her."

"It's a long story," said Nohana, beside her on the bridge.

"I have lots of tea."

"When we near your place, find a dock spot not too close," Nohana told her. "If security comes for us, this may mislead them. It's not an ideal ruse, but anything is better than nothing, and even if it gives us only a few extra seconds, that might make a difference."

"Do you do this a lot?"

"Not much so far." She pointed. "There. That looks good."

They docked in a slot alongside a public park, disembarked, and crossed the hundred meters to the complex that included Shimmer's apartment. Once inside, Nohana breathed a sigh of relief, while Shimmer kept her promise by boiling water for tea. Nohana helped her load the two infusers and set them in mugs. She wanted to explain everything, and found that she did not know where to begin. Shimmer, for her part, broached no questions, content to wait for the whistle of the teapot, for which silence Nohana was grateful.

"Honey or cream?" asked Shimmer, turning off the warmer to force the whistle to die down.

"Honey, please." Laughing, she added, "The truth is, I don't know how I like it. That tea we drank earlier was my first."

Shimmer handed her a mug, and they repaired to the bed that served as a sofa. "You must lead a sheltered life," she said, as they sat down, careful not to spill from the mugs.

"Sheltered? Not very; it had some limitations, though. I was born and raised on Cullen's Lode, out in the Fringes."

"And now you're here. Tell me why you're here."

Nohana took a few sips to steady herself, and burned her lips and tongue. "Pol and Ayvy and I... intervene now and then," she began. "We try to help people. Saving a baby who had been taken by a bird of prey. Rescuing Ayvy's mother and, incidentally, Ayvy herself. I don't yet have the full story on that. And...after getting a certain artist in trouble by associating with us, offering her a new chance at life and saving her paintings in the process." She flashed a grin. "I happen to like your artwork. But..."

Shimmer frowned. "But?" she said heavily.

Nohana pointed as she spoke. "I see a park. I see some children playing in a yard. I think that one is the patio at the *Candystripe Café*, somewhat embellished by the mood of the colors. That's a field of grain next to the edge of a forest. Shimmer, these are all local scenes."

"What's wrong with that?"

"Nothing at all," Nohana assured her. "This is not a criticism, or even a critique. Your work is good, it's great. But like my childhood and adolescence, it's limited. There's a whole galaxy, a whole universe out there. Oceans, mountains, rugged features, moons, forests, rivers, waterfalls, oh so much out there. I'd love to see what you can do with it."

Shimmer shook her head. "I could never...," she began, but was unable to finish.

"It's up to you, of course. I would never force you. But if you want to express yourself in art, I can help by being your patron, the same way it happened in the Renaissance, when people in high positions gave commissions to artists."

"Where's this Renaissance? It sounds like a good place to go."

The question stopped Nohana. It spoke volumes about Shimmer's educational background, but it also implied that her artistic talent came to her naturally, as certain talents came to a *savant*. For Nohana, continued dialogue would have to proceed carefully; she regarded the differences in their education as irrelevant, but Shimmer might be sensitive to them.

"It's not a where, but a when," Nohana said gently. "On Earth, more than a thousand years ago, after a dark period of war, famine, and poverty, the arts began to flourish again. I mentioned patrons. That's more or less what Pol, Ayvy, and I do. We find people who could use our help, and we offer it. As I am offering you mine."

"That...almost sounds as if you're asking me to come away with you."

Nohana sighed. "Yeah, it does. Shimmer, Tritonia can be an evil place, and we've just highly upset some evil people. There are more people after Ayvy than that man I killed. Eventually they will find out you were involved. Your friend Elin will tell them, if she's asked. Once that happens, security will be right outside your door, banging on it. I'm sorry about that, I really am. But that's the way it is."

"But...but you're trapped here with me, then."

"Yeah. I'm working on it. But if we're to get away successfully, we have to take your paintings with us. And anything else you can't replace. And you may want to notify someone...your parents, siblings, a boyfriend, a... well, whoever."

"I-I don't actually...like boys," Shimmer replied. "But I don't have a girlfriend, either." She gave Nohana a sidelong glance. "I thought perhaps you..."

"No, that's not why I'm doing this."

"That's not exactly no, then."

Nohana chuckled. "I suppose it isn't. But I'm in a triangle with Pol and Ayvy, and I like where I am."

"I...see. Well...I don't have anyone I need to notify, except my boss. And the only things that matter to me are my art, my art supplies, and my Tookie."

"Your...what?"

"My stuffed doggy. I sleep with her, because...well, because."

"I think I understand."

"I think you do. I can tell that about you."

"Shimmer, how long will it take you to gather up?"

She shrugged. "I don't know. Fifteen minutes?"

"One last question then: do you want to go away with me?"

The answer was immediate. "Yes."

"I could have phrased that better," said Nohana. "I meant—"

"I know what you meant. Yes!" A moment later, she added, "But how?"

"I'm still working on that. But we have to get away from *here* first. Now, how can I help you pack?"

***

"I cannot believe she did that," Cahill muttered, shaking his head. "She *knows* how dangerous it will be for her there."

"Who is she?" asked Vigdis Olafsdottir. A mug of coffee and a tin of soup had helped to restore some of her vitality. The memory of pain remained in her eyes, blue like Ayvy's, but it too was fading.

"She's...with us," Ayvy answered vaguely. As soon as the words escaped her, she made a sour face. "No, she's much more than that, Mama. The three of us are... we're together. Understand?"

Cahill cleared his throat for attention. "The word Ayvy is groping for is 'lovers.' But we're also a Unit... which will be a little more difficult to explain. Ayvy decided she wants to use her money to do something good, to help people. She sought help doing that, and found me. Together we encountered Nohana. Her cultural background...made falling in love easy."

"So why did she leave so abruptly?" asked Olafsdottir.

Cahill dragged a weary hand through his hair. "I wish I knew. She's disabled her Palmetto. I can only assume she doesn't want to talk about it at the moment. But it's certain there's already a serious investigation going on into the events we just left. When the security people or the hierarchs, or both, question that tour guide, she'll talk. She knows Shimmer—that's the young woman who was with us—and she can describe Nohana and me. They'll run the descriptions with a list of known associates of Ayvy, and they'll have our names."

"But why would she leave?" pressed Ayvy.

Cahill considered. "I think it might have been the paintings on the walls in Shimmer's apartment," he said slowly, trying to add it all together. "Nohana was impressed. And she's a...a..."

"Do-gooder," Ayvy supplied.

"Yes, exactly. She'll want to help Shimmer get away with her paintings...but I have no idea how she means to do that."

"Then we have to go back," said Ayvy.

He shook his head. "No. Our priority has got to be getting your mother," he smiled at her, "you, Vigdis, to a place where neither security nor the hierarchs can touch you. That's Cullen's Lode. No one will know you're there. After that, Ayvy and I will go back."

"The way she, and you, came for me," whispered Ayvy, as that fact fully registered. "After I behaved so...so badly." Resolve hardened her voice. "So we have to go back for her, consequences be damned."

"We will, Ayvy. I just wish she would answer her Palmetto."

***

A child's cart aided Nohana and Shimmer, and probably saved their lives.

It had been left just outside the main entrance to the apartment complex, and it meant they would not have to make a second trip back into the apartment. With Nohana pulling the cart and the box of paintings loaded on it, and Shimmer carrying the bags of art supplies and the stuffed doggy and a few items of clothing, they crossed the glideway and entered the public park, slowing their pace because there was less hurry now. A hundred meters away, the blue and yellow airfoil awaited them. Only a few people were in the park, in the shady spots under the broad-leaf trees. Staying in the bright sunlight, Nohana and Shimmer had to shade their eyes. They froze as they looked further down the glideway.

Airfoils were rushing in their direction. When two of the conveyances paused by the airfoil they had let, Nohana and Shimmer went further onto the grass of the park, hoping to be taken for picnickers. Other airfoils sped past, and stopped in front of Shimmer's apartment complex.

"What are we going to do?" cried Shimmer.

"I don't know. But we're visitors to the park. Act like it."

They moved even further onto the grass, and closer to the shelter of the trees. "I can't go back now," worried Shimmer. "And we can't get away."

"Yeah. I'm thinking. What we need is a…"

"A what? A what?"

"I wonder…"

"Nohana, *what*?"

Nohana dug out her Palmetto and turned it on. "Freya, acknowledge," she said.

"Acknowledged. There are messages."

"Disregard messages for now. Location?"

"The *Black Ice* is enTracked vic Tritonia, as Ayvy ordered."

"Yes!" breathed Nohana. "Freya, home in on my signal, put the bow three meters from me, and Fastrack."

Air buffeted them, and rattled the box in the wagon. The blow staggered Shimmer, but she remained upright. Even before the ramp finished extruding, they climbed aboard, Nohana in the lead, Shimmer now towing the paintings. A blue beam reflected off the hull of the *Black Ice*, but without effect. Another struck it just as the hatch closed.

"Freya, Fastrack," yelled Nohana. "Get us gone."

By the time they reached the bridge, the matte black of null-space greeted them in the Videx. They sat down in the captain's chairs and caught their breath. Nohana leaned back and closed her eyes, legs outstretched as she tried to relax. The only sound she heard was Shimmer crying.

"Are you all right?" she asked, eyes still shut.

"Yes. No. Oh, I don't know. Nohana, I'm scared."

"We're totally safe in null-space," Nohana assured her.

"But what are we going to *do*?"

"We'll find a place for you to do your art in peace. I promise you, Shimmer."

"I'm scared."

"I think that's just the after-effects of running for our lives. There's nothing to be afraid of now." Following a brief silence, she added, "I wonder if Ayvy stocks tea in the galley."

She got up to go find out. Shimmer followed her as if the only protection could be had in her company. Ransacking the cupboards, they came across a small box of teabags. The label identified the contents as chamomile.

Shimmer placed two empty mugs on the counter. "No teapot," she said.

"We'll use the warmer."

"For tea, the water should be boiled."

"Are you going to complain all the time we're together?" Nohana snapped.

"Are we going to be...?"

"Yeah, you would ask." Nohana filled the mugs with water and placed them in the warmer, setting the timer for boiling temperature. Waiting, she leaned back against the counter. "I'll try to explain," she said. "I'm in a triangle, a troika, a threesome. I like where I am, Shimmer. I like the relationships I have. So do Ayvy and Pol. But I don't know the rules. We haven't established, or even talked about, the rules. Is the triangle inclusive, or is it exclusive? Either way, I'm okay. But I won't risk hurting either of them by taking on another lover, not until I know the rules. And that lover will have to accept that I have other lovers. And the truth is, I'm not looking to add. I hope you understand that."

Shimmer thought for a moment. Sadness crept briefly into her expression and passed into a bit of brightness. "Well...well, at least you like my paintings. I'm not happy with some of them. I didn't capture quite what I wanted."

"There's a term for a painting you're not happy with. It's called practice."

Shimmer laughed just as the warmer binged. She took the mugs out, singeing her fingers. "Let them steep for a bit," she said, blowing on her hands. She leaned back against the opposite counter, facing Nohana. "I think what I like about you...one of the things, anyway, is that you find solutions to problems. I mean, you're smart, and you're not afraid, you do things."

"I can appreciate art," said Nohana. "I had a ten-day course, one hour a day, on appreciation. But I don't know how to capture on canvas the things that you see around you. And you're wrong on two counts. It's not a question of who is smarter. I had a more intensive education on Cullen's Lode, where I'm from. If you had that same education, you wouldn't have said that. And yes, I am afraid, when there is something to fear. I just don't let it paralyze me...at least, not so far."

"What would you have done if you couldn't get a spaceship?"

"We'd have gone deeper into the park trees, found some shrubs for cover, and waited to see what developed."

"You see? You have a solution for everything."

"Yeah." Her tone said she did not agree with that assessment. "Did you see any honey? I didn't look."

"We'll just have to drink it straight."

After they returned to the bridge, Nohana tokked her Palmetto and raised Cahill. Over his shouted concerns, she advised him of their status, and learned the *Akila* was making for Cullen's Lode. "So are we," she said, speaking shortly to forestall any more of his yelling at her. "We'll meet you out at Birdrop, on the beach a couple kilometers to the east."

"So everything's okay, then," said Shimmer, after Nohana closed out.

"Oh, far from it. Ayvy and I have each killed a corporate hierarch, and we're both wanted for murder. Pol assaulted a security officer and disobeyed a stand-down order. The three of us hijacked a corporate gold shipment. And you're an accessory to murder."

Shimmer's jaw dropped.

"Yeah," said Nohana. "Ayvy's was in self-defense, mine was the direct result of abductions committed by the hierarch I killed, the guards were following illegal orders, which got them killed, and nobody in authority wants to hear any of this. Ayvy is still the sole heir to the McKey distilleries...hmm, and that's a good question. Who's running that show now? But the rest of the charges are accurate. We did steal that gold, and Pol did neutralize an officer sent to detain him for questioning."

"And Ayvy's mother..."

"Is a material witness to some of this. But the corporations do not want her to testify, because it would put them in a really bad light. But none of this will ever go to court. I'm sure they have another solution in mind for all of us, once Ayvy signs over her inheritance." She heaved a loud sigh. "I'm not sure there's a way out of this, Shimmer. But we'll keep trying to do a little good now and then." After she thought about that, she raked the air with stiffened digits, and made a pirate sound. "When, if, we can," she added, dejected.

"At least the tea is good." For a while she drank some, and finally set the cup in the depression on the console. "How far is it to Cullen's Lode?"

Nohana smiled. "Track doesn't work that way," she replied. "In one sense, we're already there. But the astrogational computer—that's Freya—has to factor in inertia and momentum. I don't think anyone understands it, including Freya. We just know this is the way it works. In terms of realtime, though, about three hours." She tilted her head at her, the question unspoken.

"Is there someplace we, I mean, I could sleep for a while?"

"You can have the stateroom just down the gangway from mine," said Nohana. "Rest is a good idea; we've had...a bit of a day." She got up, and motioned to her. "I'll show you the way."

They headed aft. "Mine," said Nohana, as they reached her door.

Shimmer stopped, and stood very still, head down, not speaking.

Nohana sighed. "I-I told you why not, Shimmer."

When she replied, her voice was just audible. "For two, three years now, I've slept with Tookie. On some nights, she has been such a comfort. She keeps me from being alone. But this day...I would like to hold onto someone living. And to be held in return. I promise I won't...I won't."

Nohana slid the door open.

010: Councils of Love and War

The spot Cahill had chosen for a docksite was on a flat patch of sand between two rugged and weathered outcrops a couple of kilometers east of Birdrop, and far enough inland that it could not be seen from there. Both Cahill and Ayvy paced back and forth on the sand, awaiting the arrival of the *Black Ice*, while Vigdis Olafsdottir fretted over the uncertainty of her future.

The plan in Ayvy's mind was simple: give Nohana a good yelling-at, then arrange a dwelling in Birdrop for her mother, and finally take stock of the forces opposing them. The first two were set in stone. As for the third, she asked herself why and how things had gone so far awry so quickly. She knew the answer, but so far she had refused to consider it at length. To hold it up to the light for examination. But Cahill would tell her, if she asked, and he would not be gentle about it.

It's not my fault, she hissed at herself in her mind, even as she wondered why she had been so upset with Nohana and, after their talk in the clinic break room, with Cahill. Before the rescue of her mother, Nohana had been just a blip on the screen of Confederation Security, an unnamed and nameless associate of those who had stolen the gold. But now she was, like herself and Cahill, a known and named factor, wanted for murder on many if not most of the worlds of the Confederation.

Yeah, she thought. It *is* my fault.

A series of impacts on the open hatch brought Ayvy out of her distress. "They're here," Cahill called. She got up and trudged aft to the hatch.

On the sand at the end of the ramp stood Nohana and Shimmer. Ayvy had not expected them to be smiling, not with all the trouble awaiting them in the Confederation, yet there they were, cheerful as puppies among toddlers. As she descended down the ramp, relief at knowing Nohana was safe came to the fore. Ayvy gave her a hug and a kiss, followed by a long sigh as she studied her at arm's length.

"I think I have some things to work on," she told Nohana. "I'm sorry I put myself in a position where I needed rescuing. Thank you for coming for me."

Nohana made a dismissive gesture, as if she did not know what to say.

Shimmer was gazing out at the waves. "I've never seen a live ocean before," she said. "Only in holograms." She took a couple steps toward the shore. "I wish I could...I wonder..."

"What's that?" asked Nohana, following her.

"If I could use colors to capture the sounds of the waves crashing...oh, that's a challenge, isn't it?"

Ayvy stared at her. "You're an artist?"

"Synesthesia," said Nohana. "Hearing a color. Seeing a sound."

Shimmer nodded absently, her mind focused elsewhere. "Oils, acrylics, watercolors," she murmured. "Some charcoal and pastel sketches." Animated, and waving her hands, she went on, "See how the froth sprays up when the wave breaks? I think I can use that spray to create the illusion of sound as well as the motion of the waters themselves." Abruptly she whirled around. "And look at those rocks. I've got to find a way to make them speak. They're so silent, but they're really talking. I think they use the winds to carry their words."

Nohana drew Ayvy aside. "I didn't plan this," she said. "But I couldn't abandon her there. They came for her just as we made it to the park across the glideway. We had packed the things she had to take. She's going to need more clothing, and household items, and...and a house, a place for her to do her paintings. You should see them, Ayvy. And if it can be arranged so that she need do nothing but paint..." Pausing, she made a face. "Sorry. I didn't mean to gush. But we're supposed to be doing good. With Shimmer, this is a chance to do that."

"I'd like to paint you as well, Nohana," said Shimmer, drawing up to them. "If I can get you to hold still long enough."

"I'm afraid it would just wash off, the first time I go swimming."

"No, I meant..." Her face reddened. "Not what I meant. Although...hmm."

"Would you two care to move further down the beach, where you can be alone?" asked Cahill.

"No, it's not like that," Nohana said quickly, almost defensively. "It's just...for Shimmer it's the euphoria of a new world and new places to see. For me, I'm just glad we got out of there when we did."

"Maybe a thick white frosting base with food coloring would work," said Shimmer, as if Cahill and Nohana had not spoken. "It would be temporary, and it would dissolve in water. But I should be able to do a floral arrangement, with vines of, I don't know, honeysuckle or jasmine, on your arms and legs. I'll need a set of spatulas to tamp the frosting into place. The best part is that I can use the same 'canvas' over and over, taking 'graphs with my Palmetto to record each one." She grew pensive, nibbling on her lower lip. "Of course, clearing the canvas could give me a sugar high."

Undisguised exasperation and an eye roll contorted Nohana's face as she tried to change the subject. "It might be best to arrange or build—or have built—a small cottage in Bassoon for you, Vigdis," she said, holding stolidly to the immediate moment. "The soil is good for gardens, and people are generally friendly and welcoming. There's a trading post in Bassoon, and if they don't have what you need, they'll place orders with a cargo galleon that arrives every five days and delivers." Turning to Shimmer, she added, "That includes your needs, too. Canvases, paints, brushes."

"Tubs of frosting?" Shimmer asked hopefully.

Nohana ignored this. "We'll need to arrange a place for Shimmer to live as well, and transportation for her to get back and forth. You can let airfoils at the Spaceport, and I'm sure you can buy one. Or you can order one through the trading post." She paused for breath. "Okay, that's my input, and I've probably already said too much, without meaning to. I'll shut up."

Ayvy said, "Much depends on what's going on in the Confederation. Until we know more, I don't see how we can plan any permanent arrangements."

"No, I want to stay here," said Vigdis. She touched Ayvy's cheek affectionately. "I like roots. You of all people should know that. No, I want my garden, and my baking pans for bread, and...no, I'm staying here."

"I want to stay as well," said Shimmer. "But..." Deliberately she looked at Nohana.

"I agree with Ayvy," said Cahill. "I think we need to know what's happening out there. We are safe here, even if they should trace us here. Fringe worlds do not abide Confederation interference, and the Confederation needs Fringe resources. But I'm not comfortable with the idea of them knowing where we are."

"False flags for the craft," said Nohana. "False identities. The only way they'll recognize us is physically and face rec. We can set up...sorry, I'm talking too much again."

"No, don't stop," said Ayvy. "Your ideas are sound."

"But I'm not in ch...," Nohana began, and closed her mouth.

"Charge?" asked Shimmer.

Nohana wanted to pound her forehead against a tree. Instead, she tried Cahill's shoulder. It was as hard as wood, but without the rough bark. "This is a cooperative relationship," she told Shimmer. "Not that we have to agree on everything, but we do need to be told when someone wants to go off and..." She gave an anguished moan. "Which I've already violated by staying behind to help you."

"I'm glad you did."

"I'm glad I did, too. But I could have gone about it better. Pol?"

"Our most reliable source of information is Pedar Zykier," he said. "If he's still speaking with me. Why don't we stretch our legs for a while, and pull some thoughts together? Let's meet on the bridge of the *Akila* in one hour."

***

Nohana and Shimmer meandered toward the ocean. The air, already scented with brine, added a note of salt and froth spray as they drew closer to the waves. Still on dry sand, they sat and shed their footgear and socks before resuming their short journey.

Nohana's voice held a touch of disbelief. "You've never seen an ocean up close."

"I've never been more than ten kilometers outside Hamillon," Shimmer told her. "After my parents died, I stayed with a reclusive uncle for a while. I ran...I left when I was fourteen, lived out on the glideways for a while, cadged some coins, and finally found a job painting siding. I had an artistic bent, and they let me go. I've worked odd jobs ever since."

Nohana noted the gap between "uncle" and "left," but made no comment. "You couldn't resist the urge to express yourself on the side of a house," she said instead.

"Yeah," laughed Shimmer, and yelped as water swirled around her bare feet. "That's cold!"

"You'll get used to it."

"But our denims are getting wet."

"Well, there are two solutions to that," said Nohana. "Three, if you count getting out of the water."

Shimmer considered that. "I get one of the two. What's the other one?"

"Let the denims get wet."

"Oh. Nohana..."

"No."

"But...what harm can it do?"

"It might send you the wrong message."

Shimmer flashed a moue. "Wrong? Cahill told us we could be alone if we went on down the beach."

"Pol."

"Yes. Pol. Ouch." She lifted her left foot. Embedded between her toes was a fragment of a seashell. For a long moment she was so silent that Nohana thought she might be in a trance. In a way, Shimmer was, as she turned the fragment over and over, her face twisted with questions as she tried to figure out what it was. Finally she had her eureka moment.

"Something lived in this!" she cried, almost child-like.

"If you go out further into the water, you might find a live one," Nohana told her. "We call that a *scuta*. That's the creature that lives inside it. It looks like a blob, and travels by oozing forward."

"But...what's happened to it?" she asked, tucking the fragment into a pocket.

Nohana shrugged. "Something probably ate it."

They began walking parallel to the shore, sloshing through the dying waves and froth. Some of the water collected in a pool that was constantly fed by the ocean. Suddenly Shimmer stopped and pointed with a shaking finger. "That's a...that's a fish! It's a fish!"

"You've eaten fish," Nohana pointed out.

"Smoked fish, in tins. But this...this...oh, there's two more."

"Algae collects in the pool. That's what they eat. For them, this is a safe haven, where nothing is going to come and eat them. Something like a restaurant."

Shimmer saddened. "You're probably so accustomed to this that...well..."

"That it doesn't occur to me that you have a good reason to be excited?" For a brief moment she touched Shimmer's arm, taking her hand away when Shimmer looked at it. "But you're right, and I should be more understanding. This is my world, and I am accustomed to it. And yeah, I like watching fish in pools like this." She pointed at a promontory ahead, a finger of rugged rock fighting off waves. "There are more pools on that."

Shimmer did not move. She was still looking at the spot on her arm where Nohana had touched her. "If we go on the other side of those rocks," she hinted, and held her breath, unable to finish.

Nohana scuffed a foot at the wet sand. Asked, she could not have said exactly what she was thinking. An impulse had come over her, one that she had been fighting for various reasons ever since she had discovered that Shimmer found her attractive. But what was it that she found attractive about Shimmer? Her artistic ability, certainly. Her willingness to help, even after she learned that to do so would place her in danger. Her joy at seeing new things. But how were these qualities unique to her? To greater or lesser extents, and in one form or another, many other people possessed something of these qualities, and of others as well. What made Shimmer stand out?

Lyrics from a song she had heard in a movie over half a millennium old came to her, first heard in one of her classes on the history of entertainment. She did not recall the name of the movie.

"'Who can explain it?'" she murmured, not quite carrying the tune. "'Who can tell you why? Fools give you reasons; wise men never try.'"

"What's that?" asked Shimmer.

Facing her, Nohana leaned forward until her mouth met Shimmer's. Only their lips touched, briefly. Then Nohana pulled back, breaking the electric contact. Rapid shallow breathing through Shimmer's slack, half-opened mouth made her chest rise and fall under the cropped gray jersey.

"There's only half an hour left until we have to meet on the bridge," Nohana said, her regret-filled voice scarcely making a sound over the breaking waves.

"I know. It's okay."

"We all have a lot of things to decide," she said, as they headed back to the boots and shoes.

"I think the decision that matters most to me has already been made."

"Yeah," said Nohana. "It has."

***

"It wouldn't surprise me," said Ayvy, sitting beside Cahill on the bridge of the *Akila*. "Nohana is right to be so open to possibilities."

"Yeah. I just hope they return in time to hear what Pedar has to say." Cahill checked the time with Pallas. "Fifteen minutes, he said."

"Are you worried?"

"Of course. I'd be a fool not to be. We came out here to be safe, not to be exiled. Ayvy...I believe in you, and what you want to do with the money. I'm in. So is Nohana. But we can't do much while we sit here hiding."

Ayvy shook her head. "People in the Fringes need help, too, Pol."

"I don't think matters in the Confederation are going to cool down. We've pulled a Charles the First."

"A...who?"

"He was the king of England during a period of insurrection," answered Cahill. "The leaders of the uprising put him on trial for high treason, convicted him, and beheaded him. About ten years later, the monarchy was restored. Killing Charles I was unthinkable, and left England a pariah for quite some time. That's what we've done, Ayvy. We're now pariahs. We killed two kings. It doesn't matter whether it was justified. That means nothing to the other kings, those hierarchs. In fact, they'll come down harder on us, because we've hit the very-safe where they live. They know that with us around, they're not so safe. Nothing in history provokes a more violent reaction from other leaders than for someone like us to attack and kill someone who is very-safe. Oh, they'll kill each other, now and then; that's accepted. But when people like us kill them...they have to make an example of us. What may save us is that we have...well, you have, something they badly want: your inheritance. It gives us some leverage. The question is whether it is enough."

"You've thought this through," said Ayvy.

"Only so far. What I'm hoping to get from Pedar is a starting point for negotiations, a person to make contact with. Ideally, I'd like Pedar as the go-between, but he's unlikely to risk anything."

"I'm sorry."

He lofted an eyebrow at her. "For what?"

"It's all my fault," said Ayvy. "If I had just talked things out with you instead of going off in a huff, none of this would have happened. Oh, goddesses, Pol, I almost got you and Nohana killed. And you were right. You *are* right. Nohana is quite able to take care of herself. The task for all three of us is for the other two to be there for the one that could use a hand, now and then."

"I think it's about to be four," said Cahill.

This time, Vigdis Olafsdottir spoke up. "No. If my understanding of your inter-relationships is correct, and my observations are accurate, you might be looking at two triangles."

"Oh, I think she's right," said Ayvy.

Cahill was dubious. "I don't get it."

Ayvy grinned. "Precisely."

"Now you've really lost me."

"Oh, don't say that," said Ayvy, darkly serious now. "I can't even countenance losing you or Nohana. Maybe nothing does last forever, but I want our relationship to get close to it...I-I..."

"Perhaps I should leave you two alone," said Olafsdottir.

"Not me," said Nohana, just coming onto the bridge. "I want to watch."

Cahill turned around, and saw their sandy feet and the sodden cuffs of their denims. "Did you two have fun?"

"As to that, it's a work in progress." She opened the Murphy bench from the bulkhead for her and Shimmer to sit down. Their footgear and socks landed on the deck. "I suppose Zykier hasn't gotten back to you yet."

"He's now four minutes late," said Cahill. He glared at the speaker on the instrumentation console, as if to chastise it for its silence.

"Could they have tumbled to him?" asked Ayvy.

Cahill's lips tightened. "When I pointed out to him that he and I hadn't had any contact in seven years, he said that meant nothing to the very-safe. So yeah, it's possible they got to him."

"In which case they'll know you tried to raise him."

He relaxed a little. "No, in which case they'll know that someone named Paul Kipling of the spaceskip *Bagheera* tried to raise him. And if we don't have a response in the next half hour or so, I'll have to change my identity and transponder again."

"Bagheera?" asked Shimmer. "The black panther in *The Jungle Book*?"

Nohana turned to her. "You read it?"

"It was one of the very few books I was able to take with me when I...left. I've probably read it twenty times. I always liked Kaa, though. I wanted to be as wise as that python."

"When you left?" asked Ayvy.

Nohana glowered at her, and shook her head once, hard.

"I'm sorry," said Ayvy. "I didn't mean to pry."

Shimmer's gray eyes took on a faraway look. "It's all right," she said absently, and leaned back against the bulkhead.

"Incoming communication," said Pallas the 'skipcomp.

"Pallas, put it on speaker," said Cahill, adding, "Yes, go ahead."

A deep and husky man's voice responded. "I want visual."

"You, first," Cahill told him.

After a short hesitation, a ruddy and tanned square face appeared in the communications monitor. Recognizing it, Cahill gave a hard sigh of astonishment. He turned around to the others, and motioned them further back and signaled them for silence. "Pallas, enable visual to a limit of two meters behind me," he instructed. To the face, he added, "Is that better, Chair Conigli?"

"You are Pol Cahill," said Conigli. "I've reviewed your record, although there is very little in it for the past six years...that is, until the last two days."

"I see very little point in the Chair of Confederation Resources raising me to discuss a file that is no longer relevant, *M'sieur* Conigli. Perhaps you had another reason?"

Conigli sat back, and his round shoulders filled the bottom fifth of the monitor. "Very well. You and your associate have been char—"

"My associate?" Cahill broke in.

A deep frown creased Conigli's face, and his brown eyes darkened. "Do not waste my time, Cahill."

"Then let us be clear whom we are talking about, *M'sieur*."

"I am speaking of Angrboda Vigdisdottir," he replied, botching the pronunciation. "You and she have been charged with the murder of Varrell Thibodeaux, and she faces the additional charge of murder of her pastfather, Colin McKey."

"Yes, I know," said Cahill. "But why is it that it's you who are bringing this to my attention?"

"I wish to hear what you have to say regarding those charges, Cahill."

"The question of why *you* remains, *M'sieur*. However, I'll let that pass for now. I cannot speak to the murder of McKey because I was not there. However, his killing appears to have been an act of self-defense. Regarding the—"

"There are three witnesses who swear otherwise, Cahill."

"Check their financial records."

"Now what is that supposed to mean?" Conigli shouted.

Cahill's calm demeanor was a sharp contrast. "I think you know very well what it means, *M'sieur* Conigli. Now then, as to the Thibodeaux matter, he was killed during the rescue of Vigdis Olafsdottir and her daughter Angrboda, whom he had abducted illegally and tortured for information and cooperation, also illegally. At least, I've been given to understand that abduction and torture are illegal. This makes Thibodeaux's killing a clear act of self-defense, especially as he had a weapon out, had fired it once, and was about to fire it again. There are several witnesses to this, none of them in possession of unexplained funds. Now I ask you again, *M'sieur*, why is any of this of particular interest to you?"

Conigli leaned forward again, filling the monitor with his face. At some point, his left eye had developed a tic, which Cahill only now noticed. When Conigli spoke, his voice was now ominously soft.

"I can make all this go away, Cahill. I'm sure you understand me. What we want...what I want, in return, is

McKey's paper case. The combination to it would be useful as well."

Cahill just did manage to keep all expression from his face. "Pallas, mute and blackout."

"He can neither see nor hear you."

Cahill turned around. Already Ayvy was shaking her head, and had spread her hands in a sign of puzzled ignorance. He did not ask her whether she was sure. A smile of reassurance momentarily flickered on his face, before Olafsdottir spoke up.

"When they took me," she said, "they searched the cottage thoroughly. But they never told me what they were looking for."

"All right, thank you," he said, and told Pallas to re-enable.

Conigli's face reappeared in the monitor, and he was fuming even before Cahill spoke. "*M'sieur* Conigli, I have fully cooperated with you and have presented my side to the best of my ability, even though you have no official investigative authority, but I must tell you now in all honesty, we have no idea what you're talking about. We know nothing about a paper case."

Conigli bit off a furious retort, and Cahill continued before he could find his voice.

"Angrboda Vigdisdottir did rifle several of McKey's accounts for cash, but as McKey was dead and she was his sole heir, she had every right to those accounts and that cash. The only crime in all this was committed by me, and was not related to any of this. I did assault a security officer and flee from custody. I believe a fine of ten thousand thalers is an appropriate penalty. Where should I send it?"

Conigli's eyes lasered Cahill. "All the charges stand. Moreover, Confederation Security personnel are about to receive shoot-on-sight orders should you or Vigdisdottir show up on any Confederation world."

Cahill blew a long sigh. "Well, I guess we'll have to make sure we're not sighted, *M'sieur*."

A string of epithets accompanied the flecks of saliva that flew out of Conigli's mouth. "Pallas, close out," he said.

Elbows propped on the console, Cahill clasped his hands together and rested his chin on them. Warmth at his side announced the arrival of either Ayvy or Nohana. The identity remained a mystery until Nohana spoke.

"Why did you lie?" she asked. "I'm the one who killed that Thibodeaux."

He looked up at her. "Conigli doesn't need to know that, Nohana. But I gave him a credible scenario, and if nothing else it may cause a little confusion if he tries to check it. It's the only victory we'll have for a while." He turned to Ayvy. "Now what the hell is a paper case?"

Shimmer answered him. "It's like the portfolio case I sometimes use to carry around some of my paintings, to show people. Except mine is probably larger, to hold the canvases and drawing pads. A paper case is probably not much larger than a sheet of paper, and thick enough to hold maybe a ream of it."

"I wonder what's in it," said Ayvy.

"Documents, I should think," answered Cahill. "And given Conigli's desperation to get his hands on that case, I'd say those documents are dangerous to…to his corporation, and maybe even to the Confederation."

Nohana returned to the Murphy bench and sat down. "He called you Cahill," she said.

He looked a question at her.

"He got the name from Zykier," she replied. "He had to've. Unless your false-flag has been broken, there's no other way Conigli could have known. The only question now is whether Zykier gave you up willingly or he was forced."

"Either way, I can't raise him," said Cahill. He dragged weary fingers through his hair, to no effect. "I'm not…not seeing any way out of this."

"We don't have to resolve it now," Ayvy said gently. She moved to his side and rested a hand on his shoulder. "We're here. We're as safe here as anywhere. Let's work on getting settled in." She glanced at Nohana for validation, and received a nod in response. She then looked at Shimmer.

Inclusion startled her, but she accepted it readily enough. "That has my vote," she said. "Thank you for... thank you."

"And I've already cast mine," added Olafsdottir.

Hands in her front pockets, Nohana stood up. "The beach is a good place to visit, it's a good place for reverie or painting," she said. "But there are better places to settle. One of them is about fifty kilometers east of here and about twenty north. Or about fifty-four if you want to avoid the dog-leg. There's a forest with some glades, and the land is relatively flat. There's a river flowing through it to wind up in the ocean. The soil is windblown from the north and captured by the trees. It's not deep enough to till, but it will support shallow-rooted plants, and we can use an auger for holes to plant trees and shrubs."

"You've been there?" asked Ayvy.

A grin flashed across Nohana's face. "Before I met you, I was going to build a place to live there," she said. "Ayvy, may I use the *Black Ice* to go to Bassoon and place a few orders?"

"I'll go with you," said Shimmer.

"Yeah, I thought you might."

011: Shopping!

Before they stepped down onto the docksite tarmac behind the trading post, Shimmer held back. "Nohana," she whispered. "I don't have much money."

"I told you, I'm your patron. Money is my problem; capturing sounds in colors is yours, you synesthete."

They resumed their descent. "I'm a what?"

"You have the gift of being able to mix and match your senses," Nohana replied. "You capture sounds in color; your eyes can hear. And in the way you present your subjects on canvas, sometimes others can see the sounds you hear."

"You can see them in my paintings?" Shimmer asked, as they reached the bottom of the ramp and it began to retract. "You can hear those sounds in what you see?"

"Yeah, sometimes."

"Then you're a synthetic, too."

Nohana tittered. "No, I'm very real. And yes, a synesthete, to some extent. But I'm not an artist. Instead, I revel in what artists show me. In one sense or another, many of the great artists were able to portray other senses, to those viewers who were able to sense them, anyway."

"Such as?"

"The quiet madness of Van Gogh's *The Night Café*. The cries of horror in Picasso's *Guernica*. You can almost smell the perfume in François Boucher's *Nude on a Sofa*. The palpable hope you share in the face of El Greco's *Penitent Magdalene* that conveys spiritual relief and recovery from past mistakes."

Shimmer saddened. "But I don't know any of those," she cried. "I-I...I don't."

"Would you like me to teach you?" said Nohana, her voice softer than dandelion petals. "To guide you?"

Shimmer breathed her response. Their eyes met over the sound of her voice. The moment broke as

Nohana tugged at her, bringing her back to the present. "Over here. This is the trading post."

They had reached a structure of red brick and mortar, with glazed windows bracketed by green shutters, and double swinging green doors, all fronted by a boardwalk patio fitted with chairs for people to sit in and relax. Two of the chairs were already occupied, by a man and a woman Nohana thought she recognized as occasional patrons of the tavern where she worked. She gave them a nod of greeting as she ushered Shimmer inside.

There it was five degrees cooler, and Shimmer rubbed her bare arms as she glanced around, gray eyes round with wonder. She walked and touched, tentatively, like a child in a candy store seeing rich, expensive chocolates, aware of only a small coin in her pocket. Nohana followed, a pleased smile on her face. Some gifts, she thought, could not be wrapped.

Eventually they made their way to the counter. While the clerk was engaged with another customer, Nohana heard a familiar voice behind her.

"Well, Nohana, it's been a while since we—"

She spun around. "Hello, Demon."

"It's Damon," he snapped.

"Tomayto, tomahto."

"You've changed, I see."

"In more ways than you can imagine," she replied, as she looked him over. Attired in his usual style, old denims and a gray shirt with the sleeves torn off, he stood with the expectation of receiving admiration from every female he encountered. "You haven't changed, Damon," she said, placing more stress than necessary on the first syllable of his name. Her inspection of him completed, she looked around. "I think they still sell combs here."

"But I am glad to see you," he protested.

A sardonic smile matched the mockery in her eyes. "Truly? I thought you had traded up."

"It...it...she..." He swayed a little.

"Been drinking, have we?" Her tone became serious. "Damon, I've traded up, way up, and again in more ways than you can imagine."

He threw a quick glance at Shimmer, a question in his eyes, but he said nothing.

"Damon," Nohana said gently. "Go sleep it off. Go on, shoo. You'll feel better." He opened his mouth to object, but she stopped him with a gesture that also jostled the hem of her shirt a little, to expose the butt of the Singer Sizzler stuffed under her belt. "It's really better if you don't say anything, Damon."

Fuming silently, he turned away. As he left the trading post, he threw back, "I'll see you again." One of the swinging doors struck him, and he staggered out onto the boardwalk.

"You were with *that*?" asked an astounded Shimmer.

"For a while. His education and guidance didn't take, as they say. He didn't pass all his standardized tests, and he quit guidance after a year. But he said he had completed everything, and I believed him. One day I noticed his green star tattoo was fading. It's not supposed to fade, ever. It was a fake. So was he. We didn't fight, though the relationship soured. One day he came by the tavern where I was working and told me he was trading up."

"You have a green star tattoo," said Shimmer, and ran a fingertip over it.

"It means I passed all my tests, and completed my period of guidance," said Nohana. "It means I am an adult." She turned back to the counter, and the clerk who was now standing there. A white apron, smudged here and there, covered his checkered shirt and work denims. She thought his dreadlocks had grown since last she saw him. "Hello, Marko," she said. "This is my companion, Shimmer. Shimmer, Marko Coulogge. We'd like to place an order."

A smile creased his round, nut-brown face. "It's what I live for," he said, but without rancor.

Nohana laughed. "You may be sorry you said that. Better get out your Palmetto. This could take a while."

It did.

***

"We should have given her a list," said Ayvy.

Cahill's only response was a low, incoherent mumble.

She moved to stand behind him on the bridge, to look over his shoulder. "What are you doing?"

At first he did not answer. Finally he slapped his hand on the console a few times, and sat back. "Pallas is trying to access your pastfather's financial activities, but they're not there."

"You mean they're blocked?"

Lips tight and bloodless, he looked up at her. "No, I mean they don't exist anymore. At least, they don't exist where they were. Pallas is doing a search by content now, in the theory that the folder and file names have been changed."

"They can do that?" She heaved a frustrated sigh, and shoved fingers through her yellow hair. They caught in a tangle, and she had to work them free. "Well of course they can do that. What am I saying? They *own* Confederation Security."

"Not all of it. Some operatives still perform their duties impartially."

"Present company included, albeit retired," she said, softening. "I know, Pol. But did you ever think that maybe you were given that...last assignment because they knew how you would respond, and they wanted to get you out of their system?"

Cahill swore, and stared up at her. "You know...I never considered that." He punctuated this with another malediction. Her hand on the back of his shoulder soothed him.

"You're better off and more effective where you are now," she said, and bent to kiss his neck.

"Sometimes it doesn't feel that way. Effective, I mean. Better off? Yeah, by about a zillion-fold. Um..."

"Yes?" she said sweetly.

"Sliding your hands under my shirt is not exactly conducive to effective research."

"Would you rather slide your hands under my shirt?"

He laughed lightly. "Not from this angle. I'd dislocate something."

She stepped around the chair and sat down across his thighs. "Better?"

"Ayvy..."

"Yes?"

"This isn't going to work, not in this chair."

"Oh, I don't know..." She shifted position.

Don't mind me, I'm just the computer.

"I told you it might not be a good idea for Pallas to develop a personality," said Ayvy.

"Would you two like me to leave?"

Cahill nudged Ayvy off his lap, and stood up. "Pallas, you stay here and keep searching. We'll be back in a couple minutes."

Ayvy shoved him roughly. "A couple *minutes*?"

"Hours?"

"Better."

***

By the time Nohana reached the end of her list, Coulogge was weary of tokking the items onto the trading post's Palmetto. Earlier, at one point, he had grown suspicious of a prank; the amount of money she was spending was well beyond his experience. As if she were reading his mind, she quietly passed her fundscard to him and had him run the code she gave him. Seconds later, he was staring at her in awe, and continuing with the list.

Beside her, also in awe, Shimmer whispered hoarsely, "I get my own home. I get my own airfoil."

"So let's see," said Coulogge. "Two solar-powered single-dwelling prefab units with showers in the hygiene alcoves; one solar-powered prefab unit with three sleeping rooms and two alcoves, one of which also includes a hot tub; five airfoils; five hardwood desks with attendant chairs; five double beds with attendant linens." He paused to clear his throat. His voice had begun to falter, and he took a sip of water from a plastic bottle under the counter.

Nohana saved him by turning the Palmetto so that she could scroll through it, grunting little sounds of approval as she did so.

"I get my own home," breathed Shimmer. "I get my own airfoil."

"I'm sure we'll want incidentals," Nohana told him. "Now, we want the airfoils ready to travel when we pick them up here. As regards the prefabs, we'll want them delivered, and construction personnel to assemble them. Local hires only; I don't want anyone from off-world. I didn't look, but do the prefabs come with acetone window panes already glazed in, or are they separate?"

Coulogge looked it up. "They're already in."

"Appliances, water heaters, air coolers?"

He shook his head. "Those are separate."

"Add them to the list, including installation."

"I get my own home. I get my own airfoil."

"Now, when can we have these?" asked Nohana.

"If I place the order today," he told her, "the next cargo galleon arrives in two days. Most of this, if not all, should be on there; the remainder, if any, should be five days after that. And yes, we'll lay on and supervise the assembly of the units. I don't know how long the assemblies will take, but I shouldn't imagine more than five or six days, at most."

"We'll also want wells drilled," she added. "I'm not sure how many. It depends on how we decide to place the units. You'd better lay on two plumbers as well."

"Already noted."

Nohana grinned. "Run the card."

Outside the trading post, in bright sunlight, Shimmer said, "I get my own home. I get my own airfoil."

"Yes, you do," said Nohana, as they headed back to the *Black Ice*. "Now come on back down to the ground." As Damon emerged from behind the post, she sighed. "Oh, goddesses."

His hands were fists, his shoulders bunched, as he trudged across the grass and dirt toward them. Sunlight brightened half his face and left the other half in shadow, enhancing his look of drunken fury. He had eyes only for Nohana. She nudged Shimmer to one side, and stepped away from her. The grass under her feet grew on slightly uneven terrain. She shifted around until she found a smoother patch.

"This is not a good idea, Damon," Nohana said quietly.

He made no reply as he continued toward her.

"Right, then," she muttered. Now balanced on the balls of her feet, her knees slightly bent and her body centered, she waited for him. He was now five paces away.

"Nohana?" worried Shimmer.

"Stay out of my way," she cautioned her.

Coulogge came running out of the trading post, his black dreadlocks flying.

At two paces away, Damon launched a wild swing at Nohana. She threw her head back just far enough to feel the little rush of air as the fist missed her. Ducking under his outstretched arm, she rammed four knuckles into the nerve center just below his sternum, and added a knee to his groin. Between the time he began his punch and the time he was curled up on the grass and vomiting, three seconds had elapsed.

Coulogge skidded to a stop, mouth agape. A moment later, his voice worked. "Are you all right?" he gasped.

"I'm fine," she said, with a touch to his face. "Thank you for coming to help."

"You...you've changed, Nohana."

"It's the company I keep," she replied, and put her fingertips to his cheek again. "And the friends I have."

He gazed down at Damon. "He's been trouble lately," he said. "Nohana, I don't think this is over."

"It had better be," she said, and ascended the ramp with Shimmer.

On the bridge, Shimmer was subdued. The home and the airfoil forgotten, she feared for Nohana. "He looked so angry," she said.

"He'd been drinking. Ready to go back?"

She looked down at her feet. "I...guess so."

"Oh. Of course." Nohana moved to stand before her. "Freya, enTrack us, if you please. No destination, for now."

"As you wish."

Shimmer lifted her eyes to Nohana's. They now glowed like pearls.

012: On The Fate of Ilksters

The alert from Pallas brought Cahill and Ayvy out of their slumbers. Dressing quickly, he hurried to the bridge, where the communications monitor was already activated. The voice, however, belonged to Pallas.

"It is Chair Conigli. He is very insistent, and I must say I do not care for his language."

"Pallas, enable visual. Same parameters as last time."

"There you are," growled Conigli. His dark hair was now slightly disheveled, as if he had been in a rugged and disagreeable conference. "I don't like to be kept waiting when I wish to speak with someone."

"Pallas, close out."

Ayvy reached the bridge, enveloped loosely in a blue terrycloth bathrobe. A wave of caution from him kept her away from the console, and she settled onto a Murphy bench.

"I have incoming communications, same source."

"Pallas, put him on, same parameters."

"We'll try this again," said Cahill, before Conigli could speak. "What did you wish to discuss?"

For a few seconds, Conigli sputtered incoherently, before forcing himself calm. "We now know where you are," he said. "Did you imagine we would not be able to trace you?"

"Oh, dear," said Cahill, with mock concern.

"A fundscard issued on the account of Angrboda Vigdisdottir with the Bank of Relay was assigned to Ioanna Kipling, doubtless an alias of Vigdisdottir," he said, almost triumphantly. "It was used to purchase almost eight hundred thousand thalers of merchandise on Gornaya in the Fringes. I've been advised we'll have the list of specific items, undoubtedly weapons, in a matter of moments. Confederation Security personnel have been alerted."

"We won't be here when they arrive."

"As I expected. But there will come a time when you will not be able to leave before they arrive."

Cahill sighed. "And your point?"

"I want that paper case."

"We don't have it." He raised a hand to forestall Conigli's retort. "*M'sieur*, if we had it, we would turn it over to you, and end all this, as per your prior agreement. We do not have it. Let me ask you this: have you checked the enterprises of Varrell Thibodeaux? He had the most immediate interest in McKey's death, and perhaps the most to gain by it."

There was a brief hesitation. "No."

Cahill sat back. "Well, then?"

Conigli beckoned to someone nearby. A shadow fell over his face as he leaned to one side, but Cahill was unable to see with whom he was conferring. No sound emerged; Conigli had muted communication from his end. Finally he straightened, his forehead furrowed.

"It is being looked into," said Conigli.

"Perhaps if I knew what was in that paper case," said Cahill, "I might be able to suggest a possible location."

"I think not, Cahill."

"Might I ask a question or two?"

The request seemed to take Conigli by surprise, as he was on the verge of closing out. His expression said that his first inclination was to deny it. Possibly someone outside the transmission parameters was signaling to him to grant permission.

"Very well. Go ahead."

"First, what's going to happen with the McKey Distilleries?"

"It doesn't matter to me, Cahill."

"Pretend it does," he said. "Speculate, if you would."

Conigli's face hardened. "I don't see—. Oh, very well. Either the heir will sign over the inheritance, or at some point the enterprises will be divided up among those corporations that wish to diversify. Confederation

Resources has no such desire, as you might imagine. What is your second question?"

"The Distilleries are still in operation, then?"

"That's correct."

"One more question," Cahill said quickly, before Conigli could close out. "Who's managing the distilleries now?"

"Do you honestly expect me to know the personnel details of other corporations?"

"In this instance, yes."

Conigli's shoulders rose and fell, as if he were tired of the entire discussion. "I believe it is managed for now by his widow, Corallia, through their CEO, one Jass Kiribat."

Again Cahill broke in before Conigli could break away. "I'm guessing that McKey was going to do something with the contents of that paper case," he said. "Wouldn't one or both—"

Voices from the stern made Cahill pause. As Nohana and Shimmer entered the bridge, he waved them furiously to silence.

"Sorry, *M'sieur*," he said. "The café was delivering a meal. So...wouldn't Corallia or Kiribat, or both, have an interest in using McKey's plans in the paper case to enhance the business of the distilleries?"

"They've been interrogated," said Conigli. "They know nothing."

"And you believe them, but not me."

Conigli's lips pursed. "I take your point, Cahill," he said tightly.

"Then I'll close out now, *M'sieur*. My meal is getting cold. Pallas, if you would, please."

After the monitor blanked, he turned around. Nohana and Shimmer were standing near Ayvy, a bit of color to their faces, but he had eyes for Ayvy. For long seconds his searched hers. Presently he slapped his hands against the chair arms and pushed himself up, and began to pace the bridge.

"Something isn't adding up," he said, his voice just audible. "I'm missing something here. Let's assume that

Corallia and Kiribat are telling the truth, that they have no knowledge of McKey's paper case. Unlikely, I think, but let's go with it. We don't have it; you don't have it, Ayvy. Thibodeaux is dead, and his offices and so forth will be searched, but I can't see them finding the case there. Besides, if that paper case is important enough to involve Conigli directly, and Thibodeaux had it, I'm left with the impression that he would not have troubled himself over such a mundane problem as the ownership of the distilleries."

"Which means?" said Nohana.

Cahill shrugged, and spread his hands. Ayvy said, "I can't speak to the last four years, but I never saw him with such a case."

"A safe?" asked Shimmer.

Cahill gave her a little nod of approval. "Good idea. But a safe can be cracked easily enough."

"Not if it was in a bank," she pointed out.

"Ordinarily I might agree with you, Shimmer. But if a corporate hierarch wants to look at the contents of a deposit box that belonged to a man now dead, the bank would allow it eagerly. In the corporate world, it never hurts to curry favor."

"Except the Bank of Relay," said Ayvy.

"I hear you two spent some money," said Cahill.

Nohana grinned. "Does Confederation Security know you still have that device that transmits false locations and purchases?"

"Somehow it got overlooked during their equipment inventory," he replied.

"What all did you buy? asked Ayvy.

Nohana handed her a printout. Shimmer handed her a block of chocolate fudge in a clear plastic container.

"And where's mine?" said Cahill.

Nohana slipped the haversack from her shoulder. Rummaging through it, she came up with a bottle of scented body oil, which she passed to him. He read the label, removed the cap, and sniffed.

"Nice," he said. "I'll have to put some on me."

Nohana batted her lashes. "Oh, where's the fun in that?"

"It looks like we'll be living aboard the 'skips for the next few days," said Ayvy.

"We should go check out our site," said Nohana, and turned to Cahill. "Has there been any news about that paper case?"

Cahill briefed her and Shimmer. After he finished, Nohana fell pensive. She sat down in the port captain's chair, elbow on the console, hand against her cheek.

"Tell them," urged Shimmer.

They looked to Nohana, who said, "There was an incident at the trading post between me and a former lover who turned out to be a fake in many ways. Even his green star was fake. But the point is that he tried to attack me, and failed. This may not be over; he may well try something else."

"He was drunk," Shimmer added.

"But that doesn't mean he won't be sober when the time comes," said Nohana. "If it comes."

"Better give us a description," said Ayvy.

Nohana did so, but by the time she finished, a reflective frown had bestowed upon her a solemn look. "We're dealing with powerful corporations who are, I don't know, maybe trying to do something that will enrich themselves and harm everyone else," she said slowly. "I get that. But in addition, we—and people who are not very-safe—have to deal with matters that the Chair of Confederation Resources never has to face. We live in a— a what, a milieu?—where someone can walk right up to you and without a word strike you, perhaps repeatedly. I would add, strike you for no reason at all, but Damon imagined he had a reason. Because I had rejected him, and had done so in much the same manner as he had rejected me before. But when he said to me that he was trading up, I went on with my life." A smile broke through as she looked at the three of them in turn. "I'm glad I did. But that's something I was taught—that if you're open to opportunities and possibilities, they'll come to you. Be ready. Damon and others like him are never ready.

Instead, they'll attack anyone for any reason, however slight. Maybe they don't like women, or men, or people of a particular ancestry, or of a set of beliefs, or...or..."

She paused, shaking her head, with a growl of disgust for good measure. "But Conigli and his ilk—is that the right word? Ilk?—have no idea what it's like to go around with your back hunched against a blow that might or might not fall. While we have to deal with that, now and then. Some of us are stronger than others, some are more alert. Some of us want to do something, but we're not sure what it is. Conigli, for all his wealth and power, has no concept of simply living."

"He's an ilkster," said Shimmer.

Nohana laughed out loud. "Now *that* is a word!"

"You've posed a situation," said Cahill. "What's your solution?"

"Weren't you listening, Pol?" she said, her smile taking the sting out of her words. "I said I didn't know. But all right: what to do? With Conigli, you hit them where they live, in two ways. In their bank accounts, and —when opportunity and motive occur—in their very lives. You make the very-safe very-unsafe. Show them what it's like down where we are. And we're doing that.

"But in the case of someone who will walk right up to you and assault you, without a word, without warning, just because your skin is black or white or whatever, or because you're wearing a veil or yarmulke, or because they think you looked at them wrong..." She drew a couple breaths to calm herself, and looked around at them once more. "My friends, my companions, my partners, my lovers...there are over twenty-five billion humans in the Spiral Arm. I think the species is viable. Surely it can survive without," and here she glanced at Shimmer, "without some of the ilksters, at all levels and walks of life."

"So you're saying?" prodded Ayvy.

"Oh, I'm not saying go out and kill people," she replied. "No way at all. That's not what I believe. I couldn't do that." She looked at Cahill. "I know you understand that as well."

Soberly, he nodded.

"But if Damon shows up here," she said grimly, "shoot him."

013: Triangles and Shadows

While Olafsdottir and especially Shimmer wandered about the glades and the forest, the other three found suitable shade under a great spreading tree that might have been a seedling around the time spacefarers first came to Cullen's Lode. On a whim, Nohana climbed up onto a bough and sat there. Not to be outdone by a gangly sprite more than a dozen years younger, they joined her in the tree, to the protests of bird and insect analogs. A breeze from the sea, reaching twenty kilometers inland, rustled the soft leaves and brushed them against bare skin in a caress of Nature that Nohana hoped Shimmer could capture on canvas.

Legs a-dangle, she let them swing back and forth while she leaned against another thick branch. It was tempting to doze off, but she had tumbled from a tree that way before. Nearby, Cahill and Ayvy were also in a mild reverie, and she wondered whether she should talk to them, if for no other reason than to keep them awake.

"First impressions, Pol," she called out.

"I hate to disturb this place by building on it," he said.

"That's why I chose natural tones and colors for the prefab walls," said Nohana. "If the units blend with the general landscape, maybe they'll become an integral part of it. Only the solar panels will stand out a little."

Ayvy was gazing through the foliage at her mother and Shimmer. "Nohana, may I ask?"

"Oh, here it comes," sighed Nohana. "Yeah, but I'll save you the trouble of asking. Yes, we did, which is why it took us a while to get back from shopping. But I'm still...still not sure it was right."

Cahill turned to stare at her, and almost fell out of the tree. "Because?" he asked, catching himself, with Ayvy's help.

Overcoming her reticence, Nohana steeled herself. "Because I love both of you. I am committed to you, and you to me. I do not want to hurt you in any way. Yet I also care for Shimmer, even to sharing intimacies with her. But I did act impulsively—I do have that habit—and I didn't think until later that I might have hurt one or both of you..."

At first, silence followed her admission. With bated breath she waited for the response. Her heart pounded so hard that she checked her jersey to see whether it was fluttering. When Cahill and Ayvy put their heads together, risking a spill from the tree in order to whisper to one another, her heart turned to lead. She had done wrong. But...but...

When Ayvy turned back to her, Nohana wished she could clap her hands over her ears. It was in her nature to face adversity if it presented itself, but this was adversity of a different sort. It affected the heart, not the physical being. She kept her ears open.

"She's already one of us," said Ayvy. "That she is already a part of you, is frosting on the cake." Nohana could not help laughing, and Ayvy added, "Perhaps I should rephrase that."

"Don't bother," said Nohana. "I get it. But...but it's a different sort of triangle. I mean, we three are equilateral. With Shimmer, it could eventually also be equilateral, but...but not..." She sighed. "Not with you, Pol."

Ayvy shook her head. "I wasn't looking at her in that way."

Nohana shrugged. "Well, she did give you a block of chocolate fudge. If you don't want it, give it to me. Please."

"No, I think I'll keep it. I might let you have a bite or two, though." Her smile grew faint, wistful. "Nohana... if you truly love, there is no measure to the love within you. It would be difficult to love Pol and me without loving almost all people somewhat. Not that you'd go out and set records; you've too much self-respect to do that. But if someone comes along who is interesting enough, even if it's just for a brief period of time, then...well, that's where you have to decide what you want to do. You'll always be a part of the three...the four of us. Always."

"Triangles, triangles," Nohana murmured. "I must be channeling Pythagoras." She stood up on the bough and reached for a higher branch to cling to for balance. "So where are we going to build?"

"From what we've seen already, there are five sites," said Cahill. "We only need three of them. One is twice the size of the others, and I suggest we ask for that one. If everyone agrees, then there are four sites left. If Vigdis and Shimmer both want the same one...I don't know. Play Ippy-dippy, or flip a coin, or draw cards?"

Nohana looked at Ayvy. "Ippy?" she said.

"Dippy?" said Ayvy.

Cahill groaned. "Never mind. Forget I mentioned it."

"Oh, I don't know if I can," said Nohana. "Does Ippy-dippy require a hot tub, with lots of slippery bubbly lather?"

Exasperated, Cahill fell out of the tree. But he landed on his feet. "Sun's on the way down," he called up to them. "We could build a fire on the beach."

"I have a case of Warsteiner on the *Black Ice*," said Ayvy.

"Not quite," said Nohana, and grinned.

"Where did you get that?" Cahill wanted to know.

"I'm a smuggler, remember?" To Nohana, she said, "How many?"

"We just took two bottles. It was very popular in *The Blue Snooter*, when we could get it in, which was not all that often." She jumped down into knee-high grass, and steadied Ayvy as she landed. "Shall we take yours?" she asked. "After all, you've got the beer."

"And fingerling sausages in the freezer," said Ayvy. "They should be thawed about the time the stars come out. But we'll need roasting sticks."

"Ayvy," Nohana said gently. "We're in a forest."

***

Night fell so quickly on the shore that the waves seemed to rush the luminescent froth on their breakers in order to see the sand where they were to finish their journey. Even the Milky Way was slow on the wake-up call. Only the fire in the pit they had dug was enough to lend a glow to their faces as they sat around it, listening to the pops of dried seaweed and the crackle of dry logs as the flames fed. While the sausages sizzled on sharpened saplings, Nohana was finishing her second bottle and watching the interplay of the others as she sat apart from them. Cast in firelight and shadow, they cavorted now and then like the figures of early humans she had seen in the holograms of a museum diorama. At other times, they paired off for random conversations, Shimmer first with Cahill, then with Ayvy, Ayvy with her mother, then with Cahill. Mix, thought Nohana, and match. At the moment, Ayvy and Shimmer were standing close to the shoreline, with Ayvy pointing up and Shimmer standing attentively while nibbling on a small chunk of chocolate fudge. These stars were new to Shimmer, and barely familiar to Ayvy, and she wondered how many of the names Ayvy mentioned were accurate. Not that it mattered. In the night sky, a thousand parsecs from the Confederation center, the stars were free of names.

A light breeze came up, bringing with it brine and salt and a few grains of sand, and ruffling hair as it passed over them. Nohana recognized the signs but was reluctant to bring the evening to an early close. Still, out over the horizon, dark shadows were gathering, and soon enough the wind would bring them to land. In a few minutes, knives of lightning would carve the horizon, and the distant rumbles would reach them.

A voice nudged Nohana from her reverie. "A storm is coming," said Olafsdottir. She held out her own block of fudge and a plastic knife, an offer which Nohana declined with a shake of her head.

"That much, I know," Olafsdottir went on. "How bad does it get here?"

"We're the highest points on the beach," said Nohana. "We don't want to be out in the lightning. It'll be a thundershower, and it should pass within the hour. By then, of course, the fire will be out, and the rest of the firewood will be wet." Lightning flashed, and she sat up straight. "What was that? Did you see that?"

"I saw lightning."

"No, no, there's something way out there in the water. I'm sure I saw..."

Olafsdottir was shaking her head. "I don't see anything. Are you sure it wasn't the beer?"

Nohana laughed. "I'm good for four of those. But yeah, maybe it was a sea tale." She switched back to tailor-fashion and inspected the sausages. "These looked done. Where's the mustard and the dipping bowl?"

"Dipping bowl? You're lucky we have mustard."

"Never mind, I'll use my hand," she said, and squirted some into her cupped palm. "There's enough for you, too." Toward the beach she called, "They're ready."

Cahill sat down beside her. "You volunteered your hand, I see," he said, and applied the end of a sausage to it. Chewing, he gazed out to sea. "That looks like rain."

"Chew faster," said Nohana. "We only have half an —there it is again!"

This time she stood up, forgetting the mustard in her hand, which dribbled onto the sand. Eyes narrowed for distant focus, she took a couple steps toward the water. She was certain now that she saw a shape, something dark on the surface of the water, perhaps half a kilometer from shore. "It's like a whale," she said.

"Maybe it's a whale," said Ayvy, peering over the fire. "I don't see anything."

"We don't have whales here," said Nohana. "Or any fish that big...oh, it's gone now."

"Fishing boat?" tried Cahill, as she sat back down.

"They would have running lights," said Nohana. "And they would have checked the weather. They don't want to be out in this any more than we do. I wonder... Ayvy, could Freya magnify a view of the ocean out there?"

"There's not much light, but yes, she could. But Nohana...I'm not seeing anything out there. None of us are. Couldn't it be just a trick of the night?"

Nohana flopped back down on the sand. "Yeah, maybe," she said. After wiping sanded mustard on her denim shorts, she popped the top on another bottle. "To hallucinations," she said, in a mock toast, and took a few sips.

Lightning struck the water a few hundred meters away. Everyone stood up. "That's it, then," said Nohana. "Back to the *Black Ice*, everyone."

She gathered up the rest of the case of beer while Shimmer collected the sausages and mustard, and the five of them hastened to the black spaceskip docked ten meters away. As soon as they were on board, Ayvy secured the craft, and they repaired to the bridge.

Nohana went to the Videx. "Ayvy, can we get a view of the area where I was looking?"

"Do you still think you saw something?" she asked, as she gave Freya the parameters.

"I don't know, now."

She peered into the darkness. Already the wind had heightened the waves, making it difficult to see between them. Worse, the agitation had reduced the luminescence and thereby the visibility.

"There's nothing out there, Nohana," said Ayvy.

"Yeah. Yeah, you're right. Thanks for trying."

As the view returned to the beach immediately in front of the *Black Ice*, a bolt of lightning struck the sand, startling everyone. Shimmer cried out. "Aren't we in danger here?" she asked.

"The 'skip is grounded," Cahill told her. "But we may want to tint the shield. Ayvy?"

She got up, and gave the tint order to Freya. "I think that beer is starting to settle in," she said. "Good night, all. See you in the morning."

Nohana made her way aft to the stateroom Ayvy had assigned her, and discovered that she had been followed. "I really don't feel like it, Shimmer," she said.

"I'm the same way, I think. But with the choice of waking up next to Tookie or you, I would prefer you."

"Do you snore?"

"I have no idea," Shimmer replied.

"Let's find out."

014: Accused!

Nohana awoke, wondering whether morning had arrived. Beside her, Shimmer snored on, although there was a peaceful rhythm to her respiration that had lulled her to sleep earlier. Careful not to disturb her, Nohana got up and headed for the shower. By the time she finished and dried herself, Shimmer was waiting just outside the stall.

"You let me sleep," she said. It was almost an accusation.

"Sorry."

Nohana slipped past her, avoiding contact. Even so, she sensed a stab of static electricity, as if Shimmer had been rubbed with a wool cloth. But Nohana had a purpose today, and it could not be delayed by an interlude. She dug out a clean pair of black denims and a sepia camisole, and dressed slowly. By the time she had finished lacing her boots, Shimmer was out of the shower and dried, a fluffy pastel blue bath towel wrapped around her. She looked chagrined.

"I left the clothing we bought at the trading post in my stateroom," she said. After gathering up her outfit from the previous day, she padded toward the door.

"Shimmer?"

She turned back around, eyebrows arching a question. Nohana found that she did not know what else to say. She glided toward Shimmer, and pulled up less than an arm's length away. Again she felt that *frisson* of static charge, surreal but not real. She dared not touch her, not now.

"I have to go into Bassoon today," she said. "I'll see you this afternoon."

Shimmer leaned forward to be kissed, and Nohana backed away. "I don't dare," she whispered.

Eyes on Nohana, Shimmer almost banged her head on side of the doorway as she left.

Alone now, Nohana drew a deep breath and tried to relax herself. Guidance was supposed to help control hormones, but love transcended them. Ayvy, Cahill, now Shimmer. Another breath steadied her, and helped her to focus. She hoped Cahill was awake.

She found him already on the bridge, sipping coffee while he sat in the starboard captain's chair. Unwilling to occupy the port chair, which belonged to Ayvy, she leaned back against the console.

Cahill was frowning as he looked her over. "You seem serious this morning."

"I want to go into Bassoon," she said. "I can't use the *Black Ice*, because everyone has a stateroom on it for now. That leaves the *Akila*, but you'll be left without a place until I get back, sometime this afternoon." She pulled herself erect, away from the edge of the console. "So...would you take me there, please? And maybe we should let an airfoil until ours arrive." She made a little sound of irritation. "Which is something I should have thought of while Shimmer and I were there yesterday."

"Where are we going?" he asked.

"There's a docksite behind *The Blue Snooter*."

He lofted a skeptical eyebrow. "Are we out of beer already?"

She shook her head. "But not for lack of trying."

After summoning the *Akila* to the beach, he motioned for her to lead the way.

The trip to Bassoon was over even before Nohana had a chance to sit down, much less to talk with him. Breakfast was on both their minds as they disembarked and rounded to the front of the tavern. Once inside, Cahill headed for a window booth, and was surprised to find that Nohana was already past the counter and headed for the kitchen.

But she never got there. Two men in gray constabulary uniforms emerged through the kitchen doorway, followed by an older man in a pale yellow work outsuit with a white apron over it. Beside him came a woman of roughly his age, similarly attired. Both had yellow hair and brown eyes...like hers.

Nohana stopped, her eyes searching them. "Amma, Appa...what's all this?" she asked.

The taller of the two constables stepped to the fore. "Are you Nohana Dervell?" he asked formally.

"You know I am, Swen," she replied.

Ignoring the familiarity, he said, "You'll come with us to the station block. We have some questions for you."

Nohana looked past him, confusion paling her face. The metronome of her heart felt as if it were keeping time to the *William Tell Overture*. "Appa, what...?"

"Better go with them," her father said soberly. "It's about—"

"That's enough, *M'sieur*," snapped the shorter constable, who seemed to be the ranking officer, and turned back to Nohana. "Hands against the wall, if you please, and feet back."

Muttering, Nohana complied with the search. The only item she had in her pockets was her identification, which Swen confiscated. Finished, the shorter constable, whose name tag read Acker, secured her hands behind her back with a zipstrip that pressed her thumbs together. "Let's go, *M'selle*," he said.

"Not without my legal advisor," Nohana replied, as Cahill came to find out what was going on. She gave him a quick glance that conveyed nothing. "He goes with me."

"That won't be necessary," said Swen. His name tag read Saxby. "This is just a preliminary investigation."

"If you want me even to consider whether to answer a question," said Nohana, swallowing the lump in her throat, "he goes with me."

"Let's go," said Acker, and gave her a little shove.

"I'm entitled to legal counsel," said Nohana, stumbling. She looked to Cahill again for relief. His face was as grim as she had ever seen it, although at the moment there was little he could do, short of an action that would cause the Unit to leave Cullen's Lode. But neither constable was in a mood to listen to her, and she was on uncertain ground anyway, not knowing whether she was entitled to counsel at a preliminary investigation.

Only the look in the eyes of her parents gave her cause for grief.

Unable to climb into the patrol airfoil with her hands bound, Nohana was pushed by Acker onto the aft deck. There she squirmed until her back was against the stern, and sat uncomfortably while they took her directly to the station block. Shaped like a cube and built from quarried stone, it was otherwise not much different from other such stations. Steel bars blocked escape through windows, and the front door that presented itself to the public seemed innocuous enough.

Once inside, Acker led her down a hallway to a room with a table and three chairs. She was sat down roughly in the one facing the door, and left alone when the two constables exited. She heard the turn of a key in the door.

The senselessness of it all began to ooze into her mind. Try as she might, Nohana was unable to relate her detention to the killing of Varrell Thibodeaux or the gold hijacking. The Confederation had no jurisdiction whatsoever in the Fringes. In fact, these worlds beyond the edge of human civilization often served as refuges for people fleeing the Confederation, because it was safe for them out here. It was remotely possible that someone in the constabulary owed a favor to someone in Confederation Security. But paying back that favor, if discovered, risked termination, or worse.

What could they possibly want with her?

Fear and the tension of it were now her enemies. Undoubtedly the constables were watching her now from hidden optics. But watching for what? Nohana did not know. Incarceration had not been included in her educational programs. She tried to reason it out. If the constables could create a particular emotional state by leaving her alone to simmer in her fears, it might make her more cooperative when the questioning came. But what did they think she had done?

Nohana closed her eyes, and drew several deep breaths through her nose and exhaled them through her mouth, clearing her mind. Gradually, meditation took over, a blanking of all thought and with it, all fear. No sounds reached her. Respiration barely expanded and contracted her chest. Thinking herself alone, she floated in nowhere...

The inner voice resonated. But you *are not* alone. You are part of a Unit. Two triangles abutting one another to form a rectangle. You are a part of them, as they are a part of you. You cannot be alone, not here, not now, not ever...

Be you. Be brave. The Unit will come.

Sounds reached her, stirring her. A key turning in a lock, a door opening. She knew what they signified, but that failed to alarm her. Now it begins, she thought, as her eyelids fluttered open.

Acker and Saxby entered the room. Acker stood next to Nohana's chair. Saxby sat down across the table from her. He laid a Palmetto on the table and tokked it for record and for data call-up. He took his time doing so, as if to prolong anxiety. Nohana smiled to herself; curiosity was her primary emotion now. Information enabled the Unit to function. She was at this moment its harvester. Seek. Find out.

Saxby began with the basic information: with whom and by whom the interview was being conducted, the date and time and location of the interview, and the name of the individual being interviewed. Finished, he said, "Tell us your whereabouts from 1600 hours yesterday to 0800 hours today."

"You said I was brought here for questioning," Nohana reminded him. "That wasn't a question. That was an order."

Acker swatted her across the back of the head. "Answer him," he snapped.

"Such courage," Nohana said softly. "An armed man assaulting an unarmed young woman whose hands are bound behind her. It's such a relief to know that brave persons like yourselves are watching out for us."

"Shut up," growled Acker.

"Make up your mind," she said. "Talk or shut up."

This earned her another swat.

111

Nohana sighed. "This isn't going to work, Swen," she told Saxby. "I won't answer questions until my legal advisor is here with me. Furthermore," this with a glance up at Acker, "Now I won't answer questions while he remains uncharged with assault, and while he remains in this room."

"Stand down, Constable," said Saxby. He indicated a spot beside the table. "Move over here." After the grousing Acker complied, Saxby said, "This will have to suffice, *M'selle* Dervell. Two people must be present at all interro...interviews."

"As witnesses, I suppose," she said. "Your Palmetto is unreliable, then?"

"It's...procedure. Now tell us where you were."

"I have a procedure as well," she said. "Someone who assaults me gets charged with assault. Someone who questions me officially waits until I have access to my legal advisor. At this point, I would fold my arms across my chest and lean back and say, 'So there.' But I can't seem to move my hands, and there's something sticky on the back of this chair. Blood, probably, from one of Constable Acker's interrogations."

"Leave the room, Constable," said Saxby.

"I will do no such thing! *I* am the senior constable here."

Saxby got to his feet. "If you leave, I may be able to persuade her not to press charges."

Acker took a step back. "You'd testify against me? Against a comrade officer?"

"I won't have to. The Palmetto recorder is still running."

Acker stared at the table. "Give me that," he demanded, reaching for it. When Saxby blocked him, he said, "Give it to me. I know how to edit the recor..."

He stopped; he had said too many words.

"It's better if you leave now," Saxby said quietly.

After a brief but tense hesitation, Acker trudged out, and Saxby sat down. Seeing Nohana's smile, he said, "Better?"

She quickly disabused him of the notion that he had correctly interpreted her smile. "Nice charade," she said. "You get me to think you're on my side. The problem for you is that this is an interrogation room, and you're still interrogating me. You cannot be on my side."

"You're wrong."

"Prove it. Tell me what's going on."

"That's not how this works."

"That's the only way it might work," she said. "Oh, and my thumbs are beginning to tingle from reduced circulation."

"I can't release you."

"You're afraid of *me*?"

"Well, you did..."

"Did what?" said Nohana.

Saxby muttered a few words he probably would not have wanted on the interrogation record. Nohana began to understand his dilemma now. He had lost control of the interview. He could marshal facts and the speculations based on them, but he did not possess the credibility that would enable him to use them to apply pressure. The Constabulary would have to assign another interrogator. Or...

Turn that off, she mouthed at him.

For a long moment he stared at her. She breathed a mental sigh of relief when he not only shut off the Palmetto, but stood up and brought it to her so that she could verify the shut-off. He also undid the zipstrip. While she massaged her thumbs, he sat back down again.

"Acker is still watching and listening from another room," he said. "And going nuts, about now. A friend of his was killed."

"Anyone I know?" asked Nohana.

Saxby glared at her. "Don't be coy."

"Anyone I know?"

"Nohana," he seethed, and shook his head. "All right, then. Damon Faben. We have witnesses who saw you fighting with him early yesterday afternoon. Perhaps that wasn't the end of it. Perhaps you continued the fight elsewhere."

The news saddened her, as would the passing of anyone she knew. She took a moment to shake off the news, as she would a minor injury. Though she would not, could not, mourn him, she nevertheless heard a bell tolling for her.

"I didn't kill him," she said. "And if you have witnesses to that fight, then you know he swung first. He'd been drinking. I put him down, and left with my companion."

"We want to speak with her as well."

"You don't even know who she is."

"Who is she?" asked Saxby.

"No, you can't have her." She bit her lower lip.

"How did he die?"

"He let an airfoil."

"That's not usually fatal."

"You didn't let me finish. He let it, and he was muttering your name, according to the clerk at Perkaval's."

"That would still be Jedder?"

"That's right. So the question now is the same one I asked you at the first. And don't tell me it was an order. You know very well what it was."

"We left Bassoon right after I put Damon down," she said. "We went out past Birdrop, where we stayed with some friends. We lit a bonfire on the beach, we drank some beer, and we went to bed."

"So you say."

"So I say. And I have witnesses, including my legal advisor. Swen...how did he die?"

"When he didn't bring the airfoil back, Jedder traced the transponder, and then raised us," answered Saxby. "We went out at sunrise, after the storm had passed, and found the airfoil on the rocks of a promontory, Tobor's Finger, out past—"

"Out past Birdrop." Nohana shot to her feet, startling him. "What about the body? Did you find the body?"

"Well, no, not yet. We figured you had disposed of —"

"Is my legal advisor here?" she yelled.

"What? I don't know, how would I know?"

She took a huge breath, and blasted him with orders. "Go find out, *now*. If he is, bring him in here *now*."

Responding more to the urgency in her tone than to the words she spoke, Saxby dashed off. A moment later, he returned with Cahill, whose expression was torn between relief and concern.

"Thank the goddesses," Nohana breathed. "Pol, I *did* see something last night. It was an airfoil. That Damon was on it. He's somewhere out at the site. The Unit is in danger. Take the *Akila*. I have to stay here awhile longer. Go, go!"

She was grateful that Cahill did not waste time questioning her. But there would be questions; the expression on Saxby's face said so. She spoke quickly and concisely, and disclosed enough to drive Saxby into taking her in his own 'skip out to the beach site. But what he would do once there was anyone's guess.

015: Hostages

Ayvy rummaged the *Black Ice* cooler for bread rolls to warm, and found just four. After setting the timer on the warmer, she returned to the bridge, where her mother was waiting for breakfast.

"There's not much, I'm afraid," said Ayvy. Air fleeing the cushion hissed in ruffles as she sat down hard on the captain's chair. "I need to restock." She looked around. "Where is Shimmer?"

"She's out walking on the beach," Olafsdottir told her. "She's probably developing some concepts for her paintings."

Ayvy started to rise, then thought better of it. Part of her wanted to make sure Shimmer was all right, walking alone out there in what amounted to a fine drizzle, a memento left behind by the storm. Another part recalled the argument with Nohana regarding experience. Shimmer was twenty-two years old. She was walking on a beach alone.

"It's difficult for you, I see," said Olafsdottir.

The words drew Ayvy away from the Videx and the mist outside. "What's that?"

"Sharing control." Regret coarsened her voice. "He overrode your rebellious streak by demanding leadership and maturity on your part. He groomed you as his successor. He was always in charge, and it worked for him. Therefore it would work for you. And it's partly my fault."

The tears that had begun to form in Ayvy's eyes froze suddenly with her mother's admission of guilt. "How is it your fault?" she asked. "You didn't do it."

For a long time Olafsdottir did not respond. Ayvy was on the verge of repeating herself when her mother began to fumble for words.

"I had to leave," she said. "It was that, or k-kill him, or be killed by him. None of the...those options was... I couldn't, but I had to. And I abandoned you to him. I couldn't pro...protect you from...from becoming his creation."

Ayvy got up and slowly crossed the bridge to her. A gentle tug raised Olafsdottir to her feet. The embrace that followed lasted an eternity of seconds, a minute, perhaps two. Outside, the sky was weeping; on the bridge, so were they. Eventually, sniffling, they held each other at arm's length. Ayvy curled her face to the sleeve of her pullover, and wiped her nose.

"I didn't feel abandoned," Ayvy told her, and hedged. "Well, maybe a little. What I felt mostly was alone. Like the lone defender of the castle that was me. Raise my portcullis and surrender to the corporate hordes. But when it got dark, I could call on the one thing you left me with."

Olafsdottir searched her eyes. "But...but I left you with nothing of mine."

"Except your name, Mama," said Ayvy, still sniffling. "Despite all his pushing and prodding—oh, yes, I heard you two yelling about it—you never gave in and changed your name to his. You never became his possession. The one thing he could not take from you was who you are. And when it got dark, I held onto that. He changed mine on all his documents, did you know that? But on my documents—at school, at university, in the password-protected files on my Palmetto, on my bank accounts, in the written diary I kept that he looked for and never found—in all those, and inside me, my name is Angrboda Vigdisdottir. You left me with me, Mama. And it got me through."

Weeping began anew, until finally Olafsdottir had to sit down. Ayvy knelt beside her chair. "I'm getting over him," she said. "I've done terrible things because of the residue he left. I fought with Nohana over nothing, nothing! I didn't want to hear what Pol had to say about that, or about anything. I left them in a huff, *them*, the Unit of us three. Four now." A smile flickered, and went out. "Yet they came for me. They killed for me. I-I..." Her voice faltered; she could but shake her head in disbelief and in acceptance. She could but whisper. "They are everything I expected of myself and did not live up to."

"The Unit was your idea," Olafsdottir pointed out.

"The best idea I ever had. But at first I thought of it as *my* Unit. I tried to run things. It exasperated Pol, who was also used to running things. In the end, what leadership there was, that was needed, fell to Nohana. Maybe she's the compromise between Pol and me. But she is intuitive with her suggestions...and as long as we're doing..."

"Good," said Olafsdottir.

"Yeah." Her voice softened. "When it's over...when we're done, Mama, I would like to be able to say...all of us to be able to say...that we made a difference. Not a big difference, necessarily. Just...a difference. I know this much: already there are at least two children alive now who would not be alive without our...intervention. But...I have trouble squaring that up with the fact that there are people dead now—bad people, to be sure—who would be alive today without our intervention."

"The innocent and the helpless cried out, and your Unit answered the call," said Olafsdottir. "That's the morality you're looking for."

"Yeah." The strain on her knee was growing, so she got up. "I think I'll go look for Shimmer, and see how she's doing. Not," she was careful to add, "as a point of supervision, but as a point of caring. When I see her, I'll leave her alone to her thoughts." Her face twisted, remembering. "Oh, I left some rolls in the warmer."

"I'll get them. Go."

Ayvy headed aft. At her stateroom she debated whether to dig out her poncho to guard against the drizzle, and decided against. It was only water. As she made for the stern, she heard footsteps on the ramp outside.

"Shimmer," she called. "It's about time."

Shimmer's denim-clad legs appeared in the hatchway, then her face. Flashes of light reflected off her throat, and she had grown an extra arm. Right behind her appeared a man Ayvy did not recognize. In a trice, she knew it had to be Damon Faben.

With the knife at Shimmer's throat, he yelled, "Where is she? Where is that snooty, stuck-up, glob of snot bitch?"

Too late, Ayvy recalled her Krupp Narn in her stateroom. Under the circumstances, it might as well have been on old Earth. Obviously the enraged Faben had come looking for Nohana; Ayvy had no idea what he might do, once it sank in that Nohana was in Bassoon, with no estimated time of return. In her mind now, a plan began to take shape. But it was risky. Much depended on whether she could carry off her end of it. But without a weapon and without Nohana or Cahill, she saw no other choice.

In a deliberately provocative move, she turned around and took a couple steps toward the bridge.

"I'll kill her!" shouted Faben. "I swear I will!"

Ayvy paused for a deep breath. To him, it passed for a sigh, but it steadied her. She turned back to him. "You're becoming tiresome."

Faben blinked. The knife moved slightly in his hand, and a thin red line appeared in the side of Shimmer's neck. A trickle of blood began to stain the collar of her cropped jersey.

"I'll cut her head off! Where's Nohana?"

"Go ahead."

Shimmer gasped. Faben said, "*What?*"

Ayvy gave him an exasperated hipshot pose. "Go ahead," she told him. "She's just a cheap serving girl I bought at the Orphanage on Khorassey. And she's not very good. I was already planning to take her back and buy another. This just clears the books. Oh, one thing, though. If you get blood on my deck, you're cleaning it up." She tapped her foot impatiently. "Well, go ahead, get it over with. I have work to do."

The knife slowly fell away from Shimmer as he stared at her. Ayvy crossed mental fingers. *Come on, Shimmer, come on. You can do it.*

While Faben stood in disbelief, Shimmer rammed an elbow into his stomach, and fled along the gangway to Ayvy. Ayvy shunted Shimmer behind her.

"You have three seconds to get off my ship," snarled Ayvy. "You'll be dead by the fourth."

Faben got only two seconds. In the third, Cahill blasted through the hatchway to deliver a piston kick to Faben's hip that slammed him against the bulkhead. The impact drove the knife into his torso. He collapsed onto the deck, gasping. A uniformed constable shoved Cahill aside and checked on Faben.

"Help me get him onto my 'skip," he said, and Cahill moved to assist.

A furious Nohana entered, then stepped aside for them to carry Faben off. "Be careful with him," she said, acid in her tone. "We wouldn't want him to live."

Saxby scowled at her, but offered no retort. She ran toward Ayvy, who was dabbing a wet white cloth at Shimmer's wound. Shimmer gave her a wan smile. "I'm all right," she said feebly. "It doesn't hurt."

Nohana arched an eyebrow at Ayvy. "It barely broke the skin," Ayvy told her. "The bleeding has almost stopped." She took Shimmer's hand and pressed it against the cloth. "Hold this here for a few minutes."

"Would you have killed him if he didn't leave the 'skip?" asked Shimmer.

Ayvy shook her head. "I didn't have a sidearm."

Nohana looked from one to the other and back. "You bluffed...? Oh, I have *got* to hear this story," she said. "Bonfire and beer tonight. I'll get the firewood."

Cahill returned, and they assembled on the bridge. He said, "I don't know. It may have gone into his lung or his liver. The constable wants full statements from everyone, but I didn't get the sense that we're in trouble." To Nohana, he added, "You're not facing any charges."

"Yeah..."

He eyed her carefully. "Are you all right?"

"I don't know how I feel, Pol. Relieved, yeah. Angry. I don't feel sorry for him. He's a wastrel and a phony, and he only has himself to blame. I wouldn't help him if I could, and yet...yet he could recover if he made better choices. He's not evil, not in the sense of some corporate hierarchs. But he is...he's a user, Pol. He uses people. He hurts people."

Ayvy's eyes narrowed. "Are you actually thinking of helping him?"

"No. Well...no. I wouldn't know how. He had his chances, attending classes, being guided, and he blew them off. By faking his green star, he tried to take something he hadn't earned. His own failures were holding him hostage. His parents give him money because they don't know what else to do for him...something I found out only after we broke up."

"Still, it's a challenge," said Shimmer. "For you, I mean."

"To do something good?" She laughed. "I'd have a better chance of stealing the rest of Ayvy's fudge."

"As to that," said Ayvy, "you're too late."

"You ate it all?" said Shimmer, astounded. "That was a lot of fudge."

"No, I hid half of it with my mother. I knew I could trust her. And that way I wouldn't be tempted to eat it all at once. And thank you, Shimmer, for it."

"There's more where that came from. Nohana, when are we going shopping again?"

"The cargo galleon is due to arrive tomorrow," she said. "We'll have to go pick up our airfoils and whatever we get that we can load on them. Tonight will be the last night we can relax for a while."

"How do people know they can turn to you for help?" asked Shimmer.

A shocked silence followed, broken by Cahill. "That came right out of nowhere," he said, awed. "We've been too busy to consider that. Shimmer, you asked the question. What's the answer?"

Taken by surprise, Shimmer eased back a couple steps until her progress was blocked by the bulkhead. "Me? I-I...I was just curious. But...well..." She spoke slowly, gathering momentum as the idea became clearer to her. "I think what I would do is what I'm planning to do with my paintings, which is put them in a gallery on the Galaxynet, like other people do, and see if anyone wants to buy them. So I'd say set up a site of some kind...I don't know what you would call it, though. 'Help is on the Way'? 'Good Deeds Done'? 'Do-Gooders'? 'Helpmates'?"

"Oh, I like that last," said Ayvy. "Let's get it set up."

"Let's?" asked Shimmer. "You mean...you mean, with me?"

Ayvy shrugged. "I can't let you have all the fun."

Nohana headed aft, followed by Cahill. "We have some wood to cut," he said, over his shoulder.

016: The Talks

The fallen tree cut up by laser and quartered, Nohana and Cahill perched on a nearby flat rock and sipped water from canteens while they rested. Sunlight through foliage dappled them and warmed them, although already they were perspiring. The trek to the shore half a kilometer away awaited them, as did the most difficult part of the task they had set themselves—lugging the loaded wheelbarrow across uneven terrain.

Around them creatures began to stir anew, having determined there was no threat to them. Nohana knew some of their names, and pointed them out whenever she spotted them scurrying or flying about. Mimicking his remark two days earlier, she told him there would be a quiz.

"Multiple choice?" he asked.

She shrugged. "Some true and false."

He shifted his gaze shoreward. "Swim afterwards?"

She was too sweaty for her smile to pass for gamine, but she gave it a valiant effort. "After...what, exactly?"

"After shoving all this cordwood around, you still have enough energy left?" he said.

"No energy," she said. "I was just going to stand over there against that tree and let you do what you want."

"No ardor in the arbor, then."

"I might be able to curl my toes convincingly." Laughing, she pocked a knuckle on his kneecap and stood up and extended a hand to him. "Let's get this load out to the fire pit, then it's on to the shower in my stateroom. I'm sure we can find something to do there. Pol?" she finished, solemn.

"Yeah?"

"Thanks for believing in me. For coming back to help them, no questions asked." Tenderly she kissed his cheek. "Let's get moving, then."

"Okay."

She rolled her eyes. "I meant, the barrow."

"Oh. Okay."

Despite the load, moving the barrow was a one-person job, so they switched off several times along the way. Every once in a while the uneven terrain jostled a split log or two off the barrow, and they had to stop to retrieve it. Overall the labor reminded Nohana of the job she'd had loading crates of tins of smoked fish for export from Bassoon. When that work was finished, a kind of exhausted euphoria set in, usually followed by a sound sleep that night. Now, as they reached the fire pit on the beach, the euphoria that set in after finally unloading the cordwood brought back some of those memories. Attired in cutoff denims and a cropped jersey, both sodden, she sprawled onto the sand afterwards, as if she meant to remain there for a few years.

Cahill spilled down next to her, but within a moment or two he sat back up. "This was a mistake," he said.

She rubbed sand from her lips, and spat. "How so?"

"All this sand is sticking to our clothes. I feel like a breaded fish fillet."

"I'll just send out for some tartar sauce."

"Is that a frosting joke?"

Nohana spat again, and sat up, drawing her knees up to wrap her arms around them. "Every once in a while I can almost hear the gears whirr in her mind," she said. "She's accustomed to painting two, three hours a day, but she hasn't been able to do much here, yet. She's serious about frosting me. Oh, not all over me, just the...um..."

"Strategic parts," he suggested.

"Yeah. But she wants to use paint on the rest of me. I'll look like a rack of petunias."

"Nice rack."

She tossed sand at him. "It's my DNA. It said, 'There, that's the template we'll use: mandarin oranges.'" She smiled. "But I like me. I'm just right."

"Like I said."

"Well thank you, *M'sieur*." She traced a design in the sand with a fingertip, and erased it with a flat palm. "I wonder what we're going to get tomorrow," she went on. "The airfoils, of course, and getting them here will take about three hours. I'd like to start assembling the prefabs."

"Not until they pour the slab foundation."

"I know. But there must be something we can set up, just to say we made a start."

"They'll pour the slabs before they even deliver the prefabs," he pointed out.

"Oh, I know," she said. "I'm just..."

"Dreaming?"

A slow nod followed as she gazed out at the waves. "I wonder how they're doing."

"With the site on Galaxynet? It's really not complicated. Ayvy has one for her smuggling operations. The difficult part will be setting the right search words. 'Smuggling' is stark and clear. But if someone needs help finding a lost house key, they don't usually search for such help on the 'net. But gradually we'll build a reputation, and those we help will tell others about us. Hmm..."

"What?"

"Ayvy might have some connections from her smuggling days. I'll have to ask."

"I don't think her smuggling days are over," said Nohana.

"Probably not. Does it matter?"

She gave him a sidelong look. "I think some of the help we render will in one way or another be illegal," she said. "Rescuing someone from the clutches of an evil corporate hierarch probably violates a lot of laws. I don't think we should let that worry us. Helping people is the priority."

"I sense a 'but' headed my way."

"Um...okay."

"I meant—"

"Oh, I know what you meant," she replied gaily. In the next instant her tone became grave. "Pol...we don't hire out to kill. If it happens during the course of the help, that's one thing. But we're not assassins."

"Amen to that. And I know Ayvy and Shimmer will agree."

A soft silence followed, broken only by the crashing waves, until Nohana spoke. "Have you heard back from Conigli?" she asked.

"There goes the good mood," he sighed. "No, nor do I expect to. We're not welcome in the Confederation. He made that clear. Ayvy may be right: there's help needed on Fringe worlds. We'll focus there."

She got up, and offered him a hand, which he took. "Let's get this sand off us," she said. "And as much as I hate to say it, you'd better shower on the *Akila*, because your fresh clothes are there."

"There's always something."

She dashed away toward the ocean, throwing a, "Race you," over her shoulder once she had a good head start.

***

"Almost done," said Shimmer, a strong note of satisfaction in her tone. She leaned back in the chair in Ayvy's stateroom, her hand poised over the Palmetto. "We did it."

"You did it," said Ayvy, in the chair beside her. "I only offered a few nudges."

Shimmer laughed. "And a couple of exasperated sounds."

"Your idea of 'Helping Hands' was better. So was that slogan." She recited it like a barker. "Helping is its own Reward. But I'm not sure linking my smuggling site to it was inspired..." She grew serious. "Shimmer...good work."

"It's only linked to notify, not to operate. There won't be interference, in either direction." She threw Ayvy a quick glance. "Are we ready to go live?"

"Tok the magic mark."

She tapped her finger. "We're on."

"Where did you learn to do all this?" Ayvy asked.

"Oh, at the Academy. It was rough, sometimes, but you learn..."

"Academy?"

"The Academy of Life, Tough Breaks, and Survival. I didn't graduate with honors, but I graduated. Of course, the education is on-going."

"I think I see why Nohana loves you."

That startled Shimmer. "Loves? She does?"

"I seem to have spoken out of turn," Ayvy muttered, chagrined. "Forgive me."

"No, no." She twisted on the chair. "Keep spokening."

Ayvy took a moment to gather herself. She had no idea where this talk was headed, and prior to the rescue of her and her mother from Thibodeaux, she would not even have tried to find a map. The rescue had left her scarred and changed, in ways she was slowly beginning to accept. She might still make a misstep or two, but she had friends to pull her back aright. Just as Shimmer now had.

"When Pol and I first added Nohana, she had a very good education, but very little experience. She knew a lot of things, but not how to apply them to events. She had only lived here on Cullen's Lode."

"I know," said Shimmer. "She told me."

"Now she's gaining experience. I made a...one of the mistakes I made was that I stood in her way a lot. I didn't want her to get hurt, or worse. But that was not my role in this. Mine was to be there for her, not as a...a cage. And so I learned. And she is growing. Something we do all our lives. In being around her, I'm growing and learning, too. But with you, it's the opposite." Anguish contorted her expression. "Oh, that's not fair, I didn't mean...but you, you have experience..."

Shimmer laughed. "And not much formal education. I know. I was thirteen when I last attended school. I read some books, and looked at some pictures. I liked to draw. And one thing led to another. I saved every thaler I could to buy what I needed for my art. Oils are expensive. Well...not really. But on a limited budget, they are.

"So after I ra..." Ever so slightly, her shoulders began to tremble with the effort of controlling her memories.

"I'm sorry," Ayvy said quietly, and rested a consoling hand on her knee. "I didn't mean for this to go there. I know you don't like to talk about it."

Shimmer sniffed. She had shed but one tear. "No, it's not like that. I've never...never had anyone to talk to about it, except Tookie. And she only listens because she gets her tummy rubbed." At this, she gave a light laugh that abruptly morphed into grief.

Ayvy leaned closer and threw her arms around her. The sides of their necks touched, like cranes in a dance. "It's all right," whispered Ayvy, while Shimmer quaked against her. "I'm here." The words amazed Ayvy. Until not long ago, she would not have offered comfort in this way. Felt it, perhaps, but not offered it.

She pulled back a little. "Shimmer, you can tell me anything."

Shimmer rubbed the back of a hand across her eyes. "Yeah..."

Ayvy waited.

She spoke as if remembering while trying not to remember. "After...my parents died—I was nine then—I went to live with my uncle. He...drank. He didn't pay much attention to me. I came and went, mostly to school. Hardly any friends. Me, I mean. I-I...maybe Nohana told you, I don't care for boys, and...and girls didn't care much for me because I didn't play their games. I preferred peace and quiet, and I was used to solitude. I liked to look at landscapes and...

"Anyway...I was thirteen. He'd been drinking. One night he came into my room..." She swallowed hard, and found the will to continue. "When it was over, he passed out, there on my bed. I got up, and dressed. I was terrified that he might awaken, but he... So I gathered up my little sketchpad and some pencils and charcoal sticks, and inkers, and what clothing I had, and...and Tookie. And I ran away."

You should have killed him then and there, thought Ayvy. But she did not interrupt.

"I-I wanted...I wanted...I don't know what I wanted then. I couldn't think. I had a little money, but...he gave me an allowance sometimes, when he didn't drink up all his money. It wasn't enough. I-I went to two of my teachers, but they...didn't help. I don't think they wanted to. I didn't tell them everything, of course, which was why they suggested I go back home, things couldn't be so bad. You know?"

"I can't say I've been to that precise spot," said Ayvy. "But yeah, I think I know."

"I finally found a room. One thaler a night, from dusk until dawn. I could leave my things there, but I had to get out during the day. I think the idea was to force me to go out and find work. I swept out a few small shops for food and a few coins." She found a laugh. "I even did laundry, dried and folded.

"And I drew, when I could. One day I saw an art gallery. A small one. It was amazing. I'd had no idea one could do that with color. I learned the word 'medium,' as in oils, acrylics, pastel chalks...I was...Ayvy, I'd found heaven. I saw what could be done, I saw what I could do.

"I offered to keep the place clean, and they took me on. I wanted to straighten each painting every day, even if it wasn't crooked, just so I could touch it. The woman who ran the gallery was one of the artists. I got to watch her paint, and I asked questions now and then. One day I took a chance and showed her my sketchpad. She said... she said it, the drawings reminded her of, I don't know, some famous artist, who did sketches early in his career. Nohana mentioned his *Night Café*...Van something, Van Gogh, yes, that was it.

"For several months she taught me art. Not just the arrangement or layout, but how to expand and enhance my own vision. How to express what I saw. The theory of artistic expression, as well as the practice of it. She said I made her see what I saw, but what few others could see..."

Shimmer quieted again, and Ayvy sensed another transition was coming. She held her breath a little, wondering what it would be.

"It ended," said Shimmer, dejected. "Well of course it did. That's how it was for me in those days, when I was sixteen, seventeen... Of course it ended. The gallery was making no money. All it had was expenses. The art on display went back to the artists, and it closed, she was so sorry, but...yeah, but.

"I still had my thaler-a-day room, but it was getting cluttered with drawings. Some were good, others not so much, but they were mine. The day came when I couldn't pay the thaler fee, and he...he threw...everything..."

Again she saddened, and her eyes grew damp. "Nobody ever saw it," she whispered, her throat tight. Sobbing, she broke down. Ayvy stroked her arm and murmured, but she seemed not to notice. "Nobody ever got to see what I saw. But that's what I want for my art, that's all I really want. I don't care about the money, I just want my paintings, my art, to be seen. I want people to see it. That's all I want for my art. For my vision. Just look at it. See what I see, the way I see it. Look at me. I'm on those canvases, that sketch paper, that..."

She stopped for a long breath that dragged at her in and out. Her palms pressed the tears from her eyes. "I'm sorry. I'm sorry for that moment just now. Sometimes it's...hard."

"Oh, Shimmer."

"Yeah. Yeah. That was the worst day since my uncle..." She fought for cheer, and found a little. A smile flickered on her face. "But I found a job two days later. A contract team needed an extra painter for a house. It was good money, and I was able to afford a better room, and I could start over. Soon I lost that job...as Nohana pointed out, I couldn't resist doing a landscape on the side of one of the houses. I was going to paint over it, of course, but I was seen...

"But I started working odd jobs, now that I knew how to look for better work. Little deliveries, walking a dog, picking up trash in one of the parks, and even a steady job as a tour guide. Well, you know that part. But I found a better job as a food service attendant, which is where I met Nohana and Pol...and the rest is history," she finished brightly.

"And now you're starting over," said Ayvy.

"And now I'm starting...wait." Her eyes grew huge, glistening. "Am I in this Unit? You mean, I'm in the Unit?"

"Did you think otherwise?"

"I'm in the Unit," she breathed. "Goddesses, I'm in the Unit. I belong!"

"You belong."

A question entered her eyes first, then fell onto her tongue. "Does this mean...? I mean...what does it mean? Ayvy, I-I can't, not with Pol. I mean, I like him lots, and I respect him, and I like being around him, but I-I can't, it's not me..."

"Easy, now," said Ayvy. "There's one rule about that, and it is inviolable. Intimacies are consensual. There is no other way, not for us, and it shouldn't be any other way for anyone."

"So...Nohana and I..."

Ayvy grinned. "Oh, I think you've already established that," she said.

"And...and you and Nohana."

"Yes." A sliver of light showed Ayvy where Shimmer might be going with this. She wondered how she might respond.

But no words came for her to respond to. Shimmer simply looked at her. Almost at her. Gray eyes slightly downcast, as if uncertain.

Ayvy was about to speak when the Palmetto signaled. She started to ignore it, to say...something, then changed her mind. A glance at the screen identified the signal.

"It's a notice on my smuggling site," she said, and switched over. The transmission consisted of an offer. Time and place of pickup and for delivery. "It's a shipping container," she told Shimmer. "It's to go from Wallis—

that's out here in the Fringes—to Nova Lisboa on Pombalia."

"I don't know Wallis," said Shimmer. "But Pombalia is in the Confederation."

"Yeah. But the offer is half a meg. Not that we need the money, but I hate to turn it down. The catch is that delivery is to be prioritized. In other words, if I accept it, it has to be now. And it's a simultaneous offer, which means others are probably about to pounce. But we have our prefabs to set up, and…"

"Yeah. Another time, perhaps."

Ayvy's expression grew thoughtful, weighing this and that. "It's ninety minutes to Wallis," she said slowly, calculating. "Half an hour or less to load the container. Four hours to Pombalia, another half-hour to unload. Three hours or so back here. If we left now, we'd be back before tomorrow."

"We," said Shimmer, an edge of excitement in her voice.

"Well, if you'd rather stay here…"

"Wild horses," said Shimmer.

017: Whackamole

"Permission to come aboard?" asked Nohana.

Cahill waved her up the ramp of the *Akila*. He had thrown on a blue bathrobe after receiving her notice, and now added a frown of curiosity for good measure. As she reached the hatchway, he stepped aside to allow her to enter first. "Where's the *Black Ice*?" he asked, looking around the beach.

"Ayvy received an offer on her smuggling site," she replied. "She said ten hours at most, so she'll be back early tomorrow morning. Shimmer went with her."

"So it's just you and me at the bonfire."

"And Vigdis."

"The *Akila* has only two staterooms," he reminded her.

A smile tickled the corners of her mouth. "So?"

He sighed, and shook his head, a faint smile adding a couple lines to his face. She was so open with her suggestiveness, but not blatant about it. It lent a measure of romance to the repartee, and he was finding that he liked it that way. "You do take some getting used to." They moved toward the bridge. "Where did they go?"

"Out to Wallis to pick up a shipping container and take it to Pombalia."

"In the Confederation?" Annoyance colored his face as he flopped onto the captain's chair. "She ought to know better than that. And that doesn't sound like smuggling to me."

"For a half-million, I don't think she was finicky about it," said Nohana. "Besides, Pombalia is Confederation, but it isn't corporate. The population derives from settlers from Portugal and Brazil and some places in Africa. Mostly they keep to themselves. Labor-intensive society. That translates as agriculture." Slightly embarrassed, she added, "I had to look it up. Pol, it'll be all right."

"We'll have to stay fresh, just in case," he groused.

133

"If you're that worried, why not take the *Akila* vic Pombalia and wait in Track, just in case?"

"Don't tempt me."

She flashed a grin. "Why not, exactly? Never mind. I'll go make us some hot cocoa. If you have some in the galley."

"Marshmallows are in the top left cupboard," he called, to her back.

Alone, he returned his attention to the communications monitor. On the off-chance that Conigli might have something to tell him, Cahill had tried to raise him after the shower. Interestingly, the attempt had not been blocked; it had gone through, but without effect. He had no idea what that meant, but he was unable to escape the suspicion that something major was going on in the Confederation. He was not sure he wanted to be involved in it in any way, whatever it was.

A mug of hot cocoa appeared at the end of a bare, tanned arm that reached around him. A whiff of her rose-scented body lotion soothed his nostrils. He felt her lips against the back of his neck, soft as rose petals, and for a moment the Confederation itself was irrelevant, as was the cocoa. Slowly withdrawing, she moved toward the port captain's chair and sat down carefully, so as not to spill her own mug. Stretching out, and attired in her customary jersey and denims—this set dark green and pastel green—she might have been an advertisement for comfort and relaxation. But over the bridge of her nose was a tiny wrinkle, and Cahill was learning to read the signs.

"Something?" he asked her.

She made a face, and shook her head. "It's been tokking at me since the aftermath of that encounter here with Damon. Something Ayvy said about her fudge. But it won't," she dragged fingers through her hair, "won't come into focus for me, so I can look at it."

"So you feel it is significant," he pressed lightly.

"I...think so, yeah."

"It will probably come to you when you least expect it," he said. "When you're not thinking about it."

"Maybe," she said, dubious.

"Trust me," he said. "I've been there."

She sat bolt upright. "That's it!" she cried.

***

Wallis was hot. The temperature and the humidity overwhelmed everything—the thick forest that surrounded the open field and the compound, the shelving with the bottles of drinking water for the staff, even the air cooler in the office where Ayvy signed for the container. As an experienced "shipper" with a reputation—she had never failed to deliver her cargo—she expected and got half the payment in advance. She made a desultory attempt to determine the contents of the container, but nobody seemed to have a precise answer, and the foreman hazarded a guess that they were labor-saving devices and equipment. Not that it mattered—Ayvy had learned early on that those who dealt with smugglers preferred as few questions as possible. She had known without checking that she was carrying contraband before, and undoubtedly would do so again.

After she tokked the clerk's Palmetto to close the deal, the clerk wiped the sweat from her fingers off the screen. He was a swarthy older man with a scraggly beard, bloodshot brown eyes, and a habit of rubbing the side of his nose, as if he could not wait for Ayvy to leave so he could pick it, and she was none too happy about touching anything of his. But the money transferred properly, and outside she could see the forklift with the container on its forks, heading for the *Black Ice*, where Shimmer waited on the ramp with loading instructions.

There was little else for Ayvy to say at this point. Only the thalers made the encounter and the trip tolerable. With a parting wave, she left the office and followed the forklift up the ramp, plucking at her damp jersey as she did so. After the forklift headed aft toward the cargo hold, she stood with Shimmer and watched, mental fingers crossed that the operator would avoid the bulkheads along the way. They heard a clang and felt the impact as the container was deposited. The electric motor whined as he backed past the hatchway, put the forklift into forward, and rumbled down the ramp.

After instructing Freya to retract the ramp and seal the hatch, Ayvy led the way to the bridge. "Sixteen minutes," she said to Shimmer, with a glance at her Palmetto. "That'll save us a quarter of an hour. We may be back in time to pop the last two bottles of Warsteiner."

"Smuggling seems so simple."

Ayvy laughed as she motioned Shimmer to the port captain's chair. "It's anything but. I've been doing this for almost three years now, so I'm a known quantity. Even so, I sometimes have hoops to jump through in order to complete whatever arrangements are necessary."

"Do you think that clerk ever bathes?" Shimmer asked.

"I resisted the temptation to hose him down," Ayvy replied, and raised a finger. "Wait a tic. Freya, enTrack us to Pombalia, but keep us enTracked when we arrive until I've received downdock and delivery instructions."

"Your wish is my command."

"Freya...?" But null-space now filled the Videx, and she decided not to ask any questions. Instead, she said, "Let's get out of these soggy things, Shimmer, and lay out some fresh clothing, and go soak awhile in my hot tub."

"Can we take a couple chilled plastic bottles of Glacielle drinking water so we can rehydrate?"

"I'll have them ready," said Ayvy. "Meet you there."

Undressing, Ayvy thought about money. In truth, at the moment, with over five billion thalers in her accounts at the Bank of Relay—more than half of it the proceeds from the gold hijacking—she had no need for the half-million she would receive upon completion of this delivery. The Unit was well-solvent for rendering almost any assistance. But she thought it best to ignore that. At some point, they might exhaust those funds, and—if she simply got out of the smuggling business—they would regret not having availed themselves of opportunities. Besides, if she retired and stayed out for too long, she would have to re-establish her reputation before the big offers would come.

The water in the hot tub was swirling and steaming as she stepped into it. The tub was a luxury she could afford, and the soothing hot water dissolved all the stresses of the day. She closed her eyes, and cleared her mind, and before long she began to doze.

The knock at her stateroom door roused her, and she bade Shimmer enter. A fresh outfit draped over one arm, she stepped to Ayvy's bed and laid it out, all the while wearing a puzzled frown.

"Are you okay?" Ayvy asked. "You look a little...off."

"I'm fine," she said. "I just keep hearing things."

"I suppose the *Black Ice* could use a little lubricating oil here and there."

Shimmer sat down on the edge of the tub. "No, that's not it. It sounds more like...well, like kittens."

"Kittens," Ayvy said flatly.

"Almost like when two pieces of metal rub together, you know? But not quite. More like kittens."

"Meow. Get in."

"It's louder in the gangway."

Ayvy stared at her. "You mean, you can hear it in here?"

"Well...no."

She sighed, and got up out of the tub. "I don't know what you could be hearing, but if it's going to interfere with your relaxation, let's go check it out." She took a couple bathrobes out of the closet and tossed one to Shimmer.

"Oh, pastel pink," she said, wrapping herself in it. "I like it."

"Lead the way."

***

"Tell me," Cahill urged.

"Ayvy gave the fudge to her mother because she *trusted* her," said Nohana, excited. "Don't you see? It's a question of trust. Of whom you trust."

Cahill shook his head. "I'm still not with you here, Nohana."

She looked contrite. "Okay, I'm sorry. I skipped several steps in the logic trail. Get into McKey's mind. He's a domineering, bullying manipulator, skilled in passive aggression, nobody likes him, but he doesn't care, because he's in a position where he can do anything he wants with impunity. He's very-safe. He has no real friends, only reluctant associates who would squabble over his leavings if he should die. Which he did. And which he knew they would.

"But he's a very-safe. What do they want above all else, Pol? The first answers that come to mind are power and money, but you can subsume those under another heading: it's called More. He wants More. They all do. All their lives, they all want that. And somehow, don't ask me how, he's found a way to get More, and probably at the expense of the other very-safes. He doesn't dare leave it lying around, where someone might inadvertently come across it and take it, whatever it is. So what's he to do, Pol? He's friendless. Who can he turn to? Who is the one person he thinks he can trust?"

"Vigdis?"

She barked a laugh. "Oh, goddesses, no, she'd be the last person he'd trust. She totally rejected him and his life, even his wealth. But consider, if you will: he's Frankenstein. Who is his creation?"

Cahill's jaw fell open. He sat breathing through his mouth. He picked up the mug of cocoa and sipped at it, mostly to regain control. Finally he said, "You can't mean..."

She nodded emphatically. "Angrboda Vigdisdottir."

"No. No, no, she rejected him."

"Yes, she did," Nohana agreed. "At the very end. Up until then, he harbored hopes that she would see his light and return to him and do what he created her, he raised her, to do. He *trusted* in his creation."

"She has the paper case."

"She has the paper case. But she doesn't know it."

"And you got all this from a block of fudge," said Cahill, marveling.

"No, Pol," she said gently. "I got it from you."

"So the question now is—"

"Where is it? I knew you were going to ask that." Her lips tightened, and she looked disgusted. "I wish I knew. But I don't."

"You need another block of fudge."

"Don't we all." She sat back and stretched her legs out again, almost slipping from the chair. Narrowed eyes gazed across the bridge at him. "Right, then. Where's the safest place to put something, where you don't want just anyone to get at it?"

"Well, when you frame it that way, and given the relatively small size the object must be...I'd say a safe-deposit box in the Bank of Relay."

She raised an eyebrow. "Seriously? I know they have access restrictions, but..."

"Oh, these are more than restrictions, Nohana. These make the immutable laws of physics look like timid suggestions. Your money is very-safe there, your jewels are very-safe, your paper case is very-safe. That's why people involved in...questionable activities keep their funds and accounts and valuables there."

"So...how would you gain access to this safe-deposit box?"

"You and I wouldn't," Cahill stated. "McKey has to go open it. This requires that he—"

"McKey's dead."

"Yeah." Cahill had the expression of a child who had finally opened the jar, only to discover that all the cookies were gone.

"But he wouldn't have...," began Nohana, and paused, thinking furiously. "No, see, he could be tortured or otherwise inconvenienced to the point where he would face the choice of death or surrender. He would know that. He would have accounted for it, and for the fact that they might kill him. No, he would have to arrange security in another fashion. He'd...oh, Pol, he registered the box in *her* name! In Ayvy's name!"

Cahill did not hesitate. "If that's true, then she's in grave danger."

"Yeah. We have to raise Ayvy, and get her back here."

He tokked his Palmetto on the console. Ayvy's drawn face appeared, her expression remote. She seemed to recognize him. "Are you all right?" he asked. "What's happened?"

"I'm, we're, okay," she said, her voice broken. "No, we're not...not okay. Oh, goddesses, Pol."

Cahill got to his feet as if he were about to rush off for her. His heart was a tap-hammer. Fear shook his voice. Had something happened already? "Where are you?"

"We're...we're on...on our way back. Should be...be about an hour, one hour or so. I think." Before he could speak again, she went on, drawing a huge breath for her words. "I need some help, Pol. Is Nohana there?"

"Right here," yelled Nohana. "I'm right here. What do you want me to do?"

"I want...want you to go, go shopping, Nohana," she said, and gave her an impossible list.

018: "You look like you're ready to kill someone."

As Nohana entered the trading post, Marko Coulogge eyed her carefully from boots to hair, looking for signs of damage, relieved to find none. He drew his dreadlocks aside and greeted her with his customary broad smile, but his dark face quickly grew concerned.

"What's wrong?" he asked. "It can't be Faben, he's under guard and suicide watch in the infirmary."

"It's something else," she said noncommittally, as she walked to the clothing racks. Focused as she was, she scarcely heard him. Who knew, she thought, doing something good was going to include so many problems? She began pulling women's attire off the hangers, checking their sizes, and sometimes holding a shirt or pair of slacks or a dress against herself to assess her look in the post mirror. Eventually she had more than half the first rack draped over her left forearm. These items she deposited on the counter for Coulogge, and went back for more while he calculated on the Palmetto and bagged.

Shoes, boots, socks, and unders came next. These were more difficult to choose, especially the unders, which came in so many sizes, shapes, and colors. She had no appreciation for fashion, only for function, and saw no point in giving herself or anyone else a wedgie. Keeping it simple, she filled a shopping cart.

The third trip through the post took her to some simple cosmetics, several bars of soap in various scents, plus towels and bathcloths. From the jewelry counter came a handful of silver chains with gemstone pendants or intaglio cameos, items not on the list, but under the circumstances she deemed them necessary.

Foodstuffs came last. She filled the cart at random, sliding tins from shelves and topping the pile with oddments, from cocoa, tea, and coffee to herbs, mixes, and cartons of fresh milk. For good measure, she added three packages of chocolate chip cookies.

Finally, at the counter, she paused to evaluate. She nodded to herself, and then to Coulogge. "That should do it for now," she said.

He continued to study her. "Are you all right?"

"Yeah." She did not quite see him. He was a shadow, a person, a friend. "Why?"

"You look like you're about ready to kill someone."

"I am."

His dark eyes widened. "Nohana—"

"What's the total, Marko?" she snapped impatiently, and immediately became contrite. "I'm sorry, Marko. I'm...not me at the moment."

"Yeah. That look in your eyes could be distilled and used to poison vipers."

Now she looked directly at him. "That bad?"

"If you want to talk about it, I have a break coming up in...half an hour."

Reluctantly she shook her head. "I have...another commitment."

He told her the total and she passed him her fundscard. Moments later, he helped her load everything onto the *Akila*. Finished, he stood on the edge of anticipation.

Nohana fought for and achieved her best smile. "Thank you, Marko," she said earnestly. "If I need to talk, I'll Palm you."

"Please do that. You can come over for dinner. Moyra will be glad to see you."

She winced. "Oh, goddesses, I didn't even ask. I'm sorry. How is she?"

"Halfway through our second," he told her. "If it's a girl, I think I'll suggest we name her after you."

"You wouldn't!"

"I would. We've always been friends." He gave her a little wave, and turned toward the ramp. "See you."

Seconds later, the *Akila* docked on the beach beside the *Black Ice*, and Nohana breathed a little sigh to ease her stress. At least Ayvy and Shimmer had returned safely. As she descended the ramp, her gaze went out toward the breakers. Both women were standing at the edge of the water, watching the waves, with Cahill and Olafsdottir beside them. She jogged out to them.

"How are they?" she asked Ayvy.

"Cleaner." Ayvy beckoned to them. "Did you notify that doctor?"

"Genevieve will be here after she finishes with the last patient. I told her what she would be dealing with."

Eyes filled with fear and suspicion, the women began to wade shoreward through the breaking waves. Nohana counted the bathers, reaching eleven. "You said fourteen," she told Ayvy.

"Yeah."

The fact registered. "Oh, goddesses," whispered Nohana.

"Yeah."

As the women drew closer, Nohana's face paled in the sunlight. Their apparent ages ranged from mid-teens to mid-thirties. Her anger and gorge rose as she glanced over their bodies, and took in the lash marks, some recent, some older. Some of the women showed signs of bruising, especially the breasts and inner thighs. Three had blackened eyes. Two limped, and two others walked with hands pressed to their lower backs. Fighting back tears, Nohana collapsed to her knees in the wet sand. Deep in her heart she felt soul-sick. She was barely aware of Shimmer joining her there, throwing her arms around her. She pulled her cheek away from the kiss that Shimmer attempted.

"What...?" Nohana managed, and faltered. The frightful tableau before her had never been mentioned during her schooling. In dealing with it, mentally and emotionally, she was on her own.

But she was not alone. In a tone as fiercely neutral as dry ice, Ayvy said, "They were in the shipping container. It was Shimmer who tumbled to them, hearing their whimpers inside the container. We got them out. They were suffocating in there. I had an oxygen tank on board, and we gave them a few small bursts, so as not to damage their lungs any further. They were crying, they were terrified of Shimmer and me, they thought we were... and I wanted to...to..."

"Kill someone," Nohana croaked. "Oh, yeah."

"We lost...lost three on the way here," Ayvy went on, and dropped down alongside Nohana. "One died...died in my arms. I watched the life leave her eyes, Nohana. It left, and it never came back. I waited there, sitting on the deck of the hold, her head lolling on my lap, and waited for it to return, but it never did." Finished, exhausted, Ayvy collapsed against her.

"Human trafficking," whispered Nohana. Her voice became a feral snarl of murderous intent as she looked up at Cahill. "What I said before about not killing?" she reminded him. "There's an exception."

Speechless, he could but nod.

Seeing them on their knees, the women one by one knelt as well, as if to appease whatever new threat this signified. On hands and knees Nohana crawled to them, pulling herself up to one knee when she was just a pace away from the nearest. Her gaze took in each one in turn. All appeared to be of the same ethnic origin, which she recalled from her studies as something called Mediterranean. Dark-haired, most were of average height, a few as tall as she, others as much as a head shorter. All were gaunt, with ribs showing. She hoped they spoke Standard, but their suspicion added uncertainty to that hope.

"My name is Nohana," she told them, in as soft a voice as her emotions would allow her, and finding strength with each word she spoke. "You are safe with me, with all of us here. We will not allow harm to come to you. Please believe that." After a brief pause to allow that to register with them, she continued. "Now, we've brought you all some soap," she went on, and turned back to Cahill. "If you would," she said. "It's all on the bridge."

"I'm there," he said, getting up and dashing off, Olafsdottir following him at a trot.

"We'd like you to bathe," Nohana told them. "We've arranged for a medical doctor to come and treat your injuries; she'll be here any moment now. We've also arranged food and clothing for you. We have no place for you to sleep except here on the beach," she glanced over her shoulder, "and on the grass back there."

For half an instant she considered. There was no way she was going to sleep in her stateroom while these women were exposed to the elements. "I'll be out here with you," she said, and heard agreement from Ayvy and Shimmer. "We'll spread a couple of comforters for sleeping pads. It might rain tonight, but that can't be helped. But it will be a warm rain."

Cahill and Olafsdottir returned with soap, cloths, and towels. A distant poof of displaced air announced the arrival of Doctor Genevieve. The women were clearly uncomfortable with Cahill nearby, so he returned to the *Akila* and began offloading and setting up food and clothing. Ayvy parceled out the bars of soap.

Nohana watched Doctor Genevieve descend her ramp. She was a sturdy black woman in her early thirties who showed signs of having given birth recently. Her round face bore a grim visage as she approached, her medical bag swinging in her left hand. She beckoned Nohana aside.

"I told you when I Palmed," said Nohana. "They were locked inside a shipping container, bound for Pombalia as prostitutes. Obviously they've been abused. We can see, but we don't know how to treat..."

Genevieve Komolafe laid a reassuring hand on Nohana's shoulder. "Treatment is my part," she said. She spoke with a slight accent that might have come from her native Igbo. "I am concerned too of their mental state. It may be perhaps I have to take to my clinic some of them back." Her dark eyes inspected Nohana and Ayvy, who was standing nearby. "I am concerned too of your states. Do you wish I have a mild sedative?"

They shook their heads. Shimmer said, "I wish I had my oils and canvas. I would paint such a painting. It would *scream* at those who do this, and at the people who do nothing. But I will not forget what I see."

"I begin," said Genevieve, and she did.

019: Acts of War

It was the girl who calmed Nohana's soul. After being treated by Doctor Genevieve for bruises and a split lip, she was sitting on the sand just out of reach of the dying waves, gazing vacantly out to sea. Nohana guessed her age at fourteen, though it might have been younger. She made a few deliberate scuffing noises in the sand as she approached the girl, so as not to alarm her. She asked whether she might sit down and join her there.

The girl just looked up at her.

But there was something in her eyes, unusually blue despite her dark hair and skin, something in the way she looked at Nohana, that said, yes, please.

So they sat, not quite touching, just close enough to feel each other's presence, and listened to the waves speak to them, crashing and hissing and finally sinking into the sand a few steps away, one after another, endlessly. Life, thought Nohana, goes on. Each wave continues to move forward, until it can't.

She turned to the girl, and patted herself on the chest. "Nohana."

The girl looked straight ahead, eyes on the horizon. "Osmares," she whispered, all three syllables of it slow and clear.

Nohana repeated the name, tasting it. "What does it mean?"

"It is 'the seas.' It is my name."

Osmares's terse tone made Nohana fear she was losing this encounter before it had even begun. "Mine comes from an old Earth word that means 'family and friends,'" she tried again, her bated heart hopeful. "So I remember my family and my friends, wherever I am and wherever I go."

"I have no...family."

"But you have a friend," Nohana told her.

Osmares said nothing, and Nohana let the ocean speak in their stead. Long seconds passed, and became minutes, and still the girl did not move or utter another word. Perhaps words were unnecessary; they were two people absorbed in and by the ocean—a living ocean, for its waves were a sign of perpetual life. Waves had been born, lived, and died here since time immemorial, and would continue to do so until the last ray of light from the dying star that held this world in thrall. Nohana's eyes closed of their own volition, and reduced her senses to four. She heard the waves, she smelled and tasted the salt and brine, she felt the spray of foam.

She felt the girl lean against her. It was enough.

***

After some additional shopping at the trading post, Cahill returned to the beach and began setting up cots and sleeping pads in the *Akila*'s guest stateroom. He had bought eleven sets, but needed to assemble only eight, for Doctor Genevieve had taken three of the women with her back to the clinic, to be treated for broken bones and possible internal injuries. In an effort to find out what he had gotten up to, Ayvy boarded the *Akila* and wound up helping him.

"I've never," she started, and found herself unable to complete that thought. "I-I knew about it, of course," she went on. "The Confederation's dirty little secret. I knew they forcibly transferred people to work wherever needed, wherever the money was, the profit margin was. I think my f-f-father acquired some of his workers that way. So I knew, and that was bad enough, evil enough. But I didn't know—or perhaps I didn't realize—that slavery and forced labor involved...what do I call them?"

Cahill grunted with the effort of righting a cot. "'Sex workers' is the polite term," he said.

"Fuck polite. They're sex slaves."

It was the first time he had ever heard her use that epithet. Pausing, he stared at her.

"Did you ever...?" she asked, and swallowed hard. "Tell me you didn't. Please tell me you didn't."

He started on another cot. "I had one assignment that was tangential to human trafficking," he told her. "Early in my second year with Confederation Security, I had to escort a prisoner, a man who had killed his owner, and who fled, only to be captured by guards. I had to take him to the proper court—and yes, there is a proper court for all matters that even remotely involve human trafficking. It is a clandestine court, which means it's a known fact, but nobody talks about it."

Ayvy licked dry lips. "So what happened?"

"Toss me that pillow." After he caught it and lodged it on the cot, he said, "I fell asleep on the shuttle. 'Somehow' he managed to winkle the key from my shirt pocket without awakening me, and he escaped after we downdocked."

Ayvy's eyes brightened with realization. "You let him go!"

"Negligence cost me advancement," he said. "Here, flip the blanket this way. Of course, after that, I never received a related assignment. I wasn't, as they say, 'privy.' Eventually I was promoted, but not as quickly as I might have been. And I think my records included an unofficial ceiling beyond which I would not be allowed to rise. Suspicion in the suspicion business lasts forever, you know."

"I love you."

"Oh, sure, now you tell me, now that we have work to do."

She laughed. "Take a marker."

He shook his head. "I'd rather not build up an equity," he told her. "I'm not that young."

Ayvy began to laugh, much too loudly. Laughter morphed into hysterics, and Cahill swept his arms around her and drew her close. Not a ray of light shone between them, until finally, her grief and anger calmed, she drew herself away, her breathing shallow but returning to normal.

"That's why we're setting this up in here," he said at last. "The thought of those poor women having to sleep out in the rain because there are no accommodations for them...well, I couldn't let that happen. What's Shimmer doing?"

"She's in her stateroom."

"Drawing?"

"It's how she copes, Pol."

***

In the stateroom, Shimmer tore a sheet of drawing paper free and cast it onto the berth. The faces on it were too bland; she could not hear their cries of anguish in the expressions she had put on them. The faces reflected pain, but it was inaudible. It was not good enough.

The ocean, however, came to life, even in the sketch. She could hear it roar like some great beast in the mountains, from a storybook meant to make children shiver. Water tore at the fingers of rock that had the temerity to protrude out into it. In the end, water always won; the land eroded. Elation of the water reflected its continuous victory over the stubborn but vulnerable land.

But the women emerging from the surf eluded the expression of her pencils. She shifted to charcoal, and sketched a bit, but the lines of this drawing were necessarily too thick for the kind of fine expression she sought. Ultimately, her vision would be expressed in oils on canvas, but she had to get the guiding sketch ready first, to clear her mind for the colors.

"Oh, hi," said Olafsdottir, startling her. She stood in the open doorway. "I'm sorry, I didn't mean to disturb you."

Shimmer cast the charcoal stick and the sketchpad onto her berth, and sat back, stretching her limbs, mindful of the charcoal smudges on her fingers. "It's all right," she said. "I needed the break, anyway. Come on in, *M'dame* Olafs—"

"Vigdis, please." She sat down at the foot of the bed, away from the sketches, so as not to crumple any of them. "How are you doing?"

"If you mean, after discovering that the cargo we were carrying was slaves, not so well," Shimmer replied, her voice a little huskier than usual. "If you mean my drawings...I'm just not quite where I want to be. They're supposed to guide me when I do the painting itself, but..."

"May I?" Shimmer nodded, and she picked up the sketch of the waves and the women. "But this looks wonderful," she said. "I mean, it's a terrible thing to draw, but...but what's wrong with it?"

"Well...I don't hear them," said Shimmer, and hoped Olafsdottir would understand what she meant.

"But they are clearly in pain."

"Yes. I 'see' the pain in their faces, I put it there, but I don't 'hear' it. I want something that shouts out to the entire Confederation that this is a malignant evil and it has to stop."

"You want to do a painting that will get banned."

Shimmer chuckled. "Yeah. Exactly." A silence followed, while she sought her words. "It's something small that's missing, Vigdis. It's one of those little things that you don't realize is there, but when you take in the entire scene, the overall effect hits you in the gut. It's something I *can* do, I've done it before, but it's not coming for me in this scene." She thought a moment, and added, "Maybe it's because I've done so little portraiture."

Olafsdottir examined the sketch more closely, and touched fingertips to the faces of the women. "They're all so young," she murmured, from her lofty age of sixty-two.

"Yeah. Some older and some younger, but all of them are young. Age is relative, but it's not relevant here..."

"Maybe it is," Olafsdottir said slowly. "Not in the sense of age, so much, but...Shimmer, pain and anguish make you look older, especially around the eyes..."

Shimmer snatched up her pencil and the sketch pad. "That's it, that's it," she cried, her hand stroking the pencil at the paper as she began a fresh drawing, this one only of faces. "Keep the youth in the faces but add little wrinkles at the side of the eyes. That's it!"

"I'll just see myself out," said Olafsdottir. Shimmer scarcely heard her.

***

Water and foam lapped at their feet like a dog's tongue. Cullen's Lode had no moon, but the sun nudged small tides up the shore twice a day. The cold water and the jerk of Osmares's legs from it awoke Nohana. She stood up, and pulled the girl to her feet. The top of her head reached the point of Nohana's shoulder, and a light breeze tangled her damp hair. They backed away from the waves, then turned and made for the other women, now resting on the grass just beyond the sand.

"What will happen to you?" asked Osmares.

The question jolted Nohana. She thought, you've been beaten, probably raped, and stuffed into a suffocating container, and you're worried about *me*? It took her a moment to grasp that the "you" here was plural. Osmares was concerned for everyone who had helped her.

"I haven't thought about it," Nohana answered.

The girl took her hand. "They'll be angry."

"Osmares," said Nohana. "Those who did this to you and the others have no idea what anger is. But they'll find out soon enough."

"What will you do?"

"I don't know ye—"

Osmares tripped and stumbled and started to spill forward, and it was all Nohana could do to keep the girl upright. Steadied, Osmares lifted her left foot and clutched at it. A little blood was seeping from the side of her big toe. That she did not cry out spoke volumes to Nohana: the girl was so accustomed to pain that it no longer seemed worthwhile to complain about it.

Nohana turned back, her eyes scanning the sand for whatever Osmares's foot might have struck. The girl looked too, and soon found a rough finger of something protruding just a couple centimeters out of the sand. It seemed to be made of reddish-brown glass, and when she wrapped her fingers around it to pull it out, the rough edges cut her. She examined her hand for a moment, and wiped the blood on her denim shorts.

"What," asked Nohana, not expecting an answer, "is that?"

Both of them got down on their knees and started pushing loose sand away from the object, careful not to come into contact with it. Soon they had excavated a moat around it, deep enough to reach some damp sand above the water table. Removing even more sand allowed water to seep into the moat. The girl took her shirt off and wrapped it around her hand, and pushed and pulled at what was now a slightly curved protrusion of glass that was browner toward the lower end. It seemed to be coming loose. Finally, with one great push, Osmares made it collapse into the moat.

Curved, reddish-brown to brown, and about five or six centimeters in diameter, it featured rough and sharp edges all around it and up and down its length. The bottom of it expanded to almost twenty centimeters, and provided support when Osmares stood it on the sand. It reminded Nohana of some creature emerging from the sand, or perhaps an upthrust of glassy rock fed from a well of it below. She had no idea what it was.

Osmares, however, wore a look of rapt fascination. She got to her feet, wrapped her shirt around the rock, and lifted it, being careful not to let it touch her skin. She could not have been clearer regarding her intent if she had simply said, "Mine."

Nohana wondered what the girl was going to do with it.

020: Job Search

The night passed as nights have done since worlds began rotating on their axes. Between the gray and the darkness there came sleep, sometimes interrupted by stretches of illuminated activity, some of them in color. These usually faded back to darkness, but a sound woke Nohana. It was a steady two-toned sound, louder then softer, like respiration. But it wasn't hers.

"Lights ten percent," said Nohana, and sat up.

Osmares was sleeping on her left side on the deck, facing the berth, her knees bent, both hands flat to pillow her cheek. In the dim light her slack face appeared angelic. In repose, she looked closer to twelve, and not the fourteen of Nohana's original estimate. A pale jersey at least three sizes too large encased her gaunt body to mid-thigh. Except for the bandage on her big toe, her feet were bare.

The sandglass object they had found on the beach stood within arm's reach of her head, still wrapped in the shirt she had sacrificed.

"Goddesses," whispered Nohana. When you live in fear, she thought, you sleep where you think it's safe, even if uncomfortable...if you can find such a place.

She bent down and nudged the girl, who awoke with a start, eyes huge with fright. "It's just me," Nohana said quickly, as Osmares scrambled to her feet and began backing away. "Nohana, remember? Friend?"

Osmares stopped. Seconds passed before she nodded hesitantly, blinking at last as she recovered from whatever she had been dreaming.

Nohana patted the pad beside her. "Come, sit down," she said, a plea in her tone. "Next to me."

The girl obeyed, to a point. Instead of sitting on the bed, she stopped directly in front of Nohana, poised now, but uncertain. Intuitive, Nohana held out her arms, and Osmares collapsed into the hug. For a long time she stood there, clinging to Nohana like a limpet, making no sound at all, her thin chest trembling, but barely rising and falling with each breath she drew. Nohana wondered whether she had fallen back into sleep.

Presently Nohana gently nudged her, and held her away. "What is it?" she asked, looking the girl over. "What's wrong?"

"Sc-scared."

"Oh, baby, there's nothing to be afraid of."

"Outside..."

"You mean the storm? It's just rain and thunder. It will pass." She shifted Osmares to one side. "Here, sit up here with me," she said.

The girl climbed up, and sat like Nohana, with legs dangling. Her feet just did reach the deck. She folded her hands in her lap.

"Better?" asked Nohana.

Osmares nodded.

"Would you like to talk?"

The girl considered, and shook her head.

"Did you want to sleep in here with me?"

"Yes," Osmares replied.

Nohana laughed. "Well, I'm not sleeping on the deck, so I guess you'll have to sleep up here, too."

The corners of Osmares's mouth twitched upwards, just a little, as if she were afraid to show too much happiness. Nohana had to close her eyes to this. Behind her lids, a possibility began to take form, and she knew she was on the verge of adding another path to the ones she already trod. Yeah, she thought, and opened her eyes.

"Osmares, do you know what I've never had?"

The girl shook her head.

"I've never had a sister."

Osmares's face said that she had not expected that response. For a moment, she gazed down at her bare feet. She started to speak then, but turned her face to Nohana to confront her with the request.

"Can I be your sister?"

"I would like that very, very much."

Nohana laid back, and stretched out her right arm. "Put your head on my shoulder," she said. "And go to sleep. I'll be right here with you. And you will be safe, Osmares, I promise you will."

The girl nestled alongside her. Within a minute she was fast asleep.

Nohana darkened the room, and lay with eyes open to gaze at the overhead, though she could not see it now. Her thoughts continued outward, through the hull, past the night sky, and out into the Universe...

***

The next morning, having decided that one of them should stay behind with the women while the others went to the trading post for the airfoils and whatever else had arrived on the cargo galleon, they drew cards from a deck. The Fates intervened: Vigdis Olafsdottir drew a trey. Though she wanted to go with them, her experience and the fact that she was a little older and worth listening to made her the logical candidate to watch over the others.

At the trading post, Nohana was able to change the order for the triad's prefab from three sleeping rooms to four. Osmares, as persistent as a proverbial little lamb, remained by her side during this adjustment. Tears lurked in the corners of her eyes as she listened to Nohana introduce her to Coulogge as her sister, a status that he accepted without question.

The lurking tears plummeted when Nohana said, "That other sleeping room is for you, Osmares. That's your room."

There followed a burst of shopping. Clothes and shoes that fit. A bar of soap the girl sniffed and wanted to smell like. Items of personal hygiene. A box of modeling clay in various colors. A Palmetto with local communication range. And a very small block of fudge. Most of these they stowed aboard the *Akila*.

The fudge, however, did not make it out the door.

Under the watchful eye of Cahill and Ayvy, workers from the trading post uncrated the airfoils and put them in operating condition, a process that ate up an hour of the morning. Assisting them at times and supervising at others, Wren Peccatto, the owner and manager of the trading post, reviewed with Cahill what had arrived this day and what remained pending. Peccatto was a beefy man with a missing upper incisor, a nose that had been broken on at least two occasions, and a history in the Confederation. With money from ill-gotten gains—he had never disclosed the source—he had fled to the Fringes, to Cullen's Lode, and there, almost twenty years ago, had purchased a majority holding in the trading post. Activating a latent talent for organization, personnel management, and profitability-recognition, he eventually had acquired full ownership of the post, but had the good sense to retain most of those individuals who had been running the place before his arrival. The continuity served to make the post the center for commerce not only in Bassoon but for Cullen's Lode itself.

"They'll be out to lay the forms for the slabs late this afternoon," he told Cahill, while his people verified that the solar cells were fully charged and test-flew the airfoils around Bassoon. "Depending on the weather, we'll pour the slabs either this evening or tomorrow morning. Rain won't affect the plasticrete, but it would bother the workers if it's pouring down hard on them. We'll keep the appliances here, but hook them up to test them. Anything that won't function will be returned and replaced, but that's rarely necessary. Fringe manufacturing doesn't just meet specifications, it exceeds them. Do you want us to unpack the miscellany boxes and crates, too?"

"No," said Cahill. "We'll do that out at the site. But maybe we could let some waterproof canvas to keep the rain off them?"

Peccatto signaled to one of the women working on the airfoils, and gave her instructions.

"What about the wells?" asked Ayvy.

"It will only take a couple hours to drill and set the pipes," Peccatto told her. "Maybe three at the outside. We'll do it tomorrow morning, after we pour the slabs, if we have to do that then."

Ayvy heaved the sigh of one who had finally reached a decision. Carefully she said, "*M'sieur* Peccatto, are—"

"Wren," he corrected her, laughing. He did not appear shy about his missing tooth. "With the amount of money you folks are spending, you can call me anything you want."

"Wren, are you hiring?"

He turned to regard her. "Are you looking for work?"

She shook her head. "Not for me, no." She told him about the women she and Shimmer had rescued.

When she had finished, Peccatto blew a long sigh. "We're probably talking about unskilled labor here," he said. His tone added that he was not quite willing to turn her down, but.

"Probably," Ayvy agreed. "And I don't actually know if any of them would want a job here."

"Understood." He dragged the thick fingers of both hands through tangles in his long black hair. "Cleaning the floors and the hygiene alcoves. Cleaning up spills and that. Maybe restocking some items. It would be living wages if they're frugal." He drew a short breath. "Let's say two, maximum. They can probably share a room above the tavern or at the *Alloggio* to save lodging money, and take meals there."

"Let's say you pay them thirty percent above what you're thinking," said Ayvy.

He shook his head. "I can't afford that, not for unskilled."

"You don't have to. I'll pay the additional to you, you pay it to them."

"Why make me the middleman?" he asked. "Why not just pay it to them direc...oh. Of course."

"Right. These women need to feel good about themselves, Wren. They need some pride. I'm not saying don't scold them if they mess up, you should know that. But at the end of the day, when they get paid...well, you know what it's like to have money you've earned."

His own background in questionable activities made him laugh. Her expression said that she knew why.

"All right," he said. "But I'm not taking them on faith. If they can't or won't do the work, I'll have to let them go."

Several airfoils were hovering beside the dock in the sheltered inlet, while a few men and women loaded plastic crates onto them. Despite the moderate pace, it was sweat work, and the loaders were lightly dressed in drenched clothing and scuffed boots. A forklift was available, but was useless for loading pallets directly onto airfoils; that work had to be done by hand.

Shimmer watched them with an artist's eye and with an eye filled with general curiosity. She stood at the land end of the pier, to one side and out of the way of the workers. Sunlight made her wish she had bought a hat, and had worn cooler attire. Every once in a while a worker out on the dock would pause, and take a drink of chilled water from a plastic bottle kept in a cooler there. A sign on the cooler read Bassoon Cannery.

"Are you here looking for work?"

The voice was female but somewhat deep, as if she often spoke loudly. Shimmer turned to see a sturdy and well-tanned woman more toward Olafsdottir's age than her own. She was wearing a thin white shirt and tan denims and brown work boots. Her sun-bleached brown hair was done up in a chignon, although a few strands of it blew in the intermittent breeze that wafted in from the ocean. She regarded Shimmer expectantly.

Shimmer shook her head. "I was just watching to see what Nohana Dervell used to do here. I'm sorry if I'm in the way."

"You're not." The woman's name tag read Malley, but Shimmer had no idea whether that was a first or last name. "She quit about three months ago. Do you know her?"

Shimmer kept it simple. "Yes."

"If you see her, tell her we'd like her back."

"Yeah..." Malley started to move on, but a mad notion dashed across Shimmer's thoughts, and she said, "Wait. Are you hiring?"

Malley turned back. "Me?" Now she inspected Shimmer with different eyes. "I'm just a shift supervisor," she said. "But the cannery owner listens to my recommendations. But I though you said you weren't looking."

"Do you have a moment?"

Malley watched the loading for a while, and what she saw on the docks seemed to satisfy her for the time being. "Go ahead," she said. "But don't take too long."

Shimmer explained about the women she and Ayvy had rescued.

After she finished, Malley swore, and added, "Goddesses," for good measure. Again she regarded Shimmer in a new light. "That must have been traumatic for you as well," she said.

"I...yeah, but..." She took a deep breath. "*M'selle* Malley, I'm not sure any of them would want to work here. Most of them are not in good physical condition. But if you could find work for one or even two of them, maybe part-time, until they build up their strength..."

"Bring them here tomorrow at eight," said Malley. "But part-time isn't going to pay them all that much."

"I know. But it's a start. It's the way I started." She hesitated briefly. "I'm not actually from here, you know—"

"The way you're dressed in this heat," she said drily, "I would never have guessed."

Shimmer laughed. "I'm a quick study; I'll adapt. *M'selle* Malley, is there someplace they could stay where it's not too expensive?"

"Try the *Alloggio*," she said. "It's cheap, it's clean, and a few of these people stay there as well. And they can take meals there."

"Thank you."

Malley turned to leave. "If they show up, I'll put them to work."

In *The Blue Snooter*, the mid-day crowd had dissipated, leaving Nohana sitting with Osmares in a window booth, sipping lemonade. Every few seconds

Nohana glanced toward the kitchen, to see whether her parents were finished with their preparations for the evening meal. In one of the moments when she wasn't looking, they came to her booth and sat down. Relief shone in their brown eyes and in their overall expressions. Her mother reached across the table for Nohana's hand and clung to it as if to never let her go.

One of the serving girls approached and poured coffee for her parents. Her father said, "I think we've heard all the spurious rumors, Nohana. But what in the stars happened?"

Nohana gave them an abridged version, with just enough information to be satisfying. "I keep looking at it this way and that, Appa, to see if there was something I might have done differently. But I know this was not my fault. He made his choices. I defended myself. That's what it comes down to."

"You've changed since you went off with your... friends," he said. "I had no idea you were able to...well, there's no other word for it. To fight."

"To defend myself, Appa," Nohana replied. "Not to attack people."

"I'm glad you're all right," he said, less severely.

Her mother nodded, and regarded Osmares thoughtfully. "You look awfully young," she said to her, and turned to Nohana. "Has she been guided? Or are you guiding her?"

"No, Amma, that's not it at all," said Nohana, and rendered them another abridged version of events, choosing her words deliberately to avoid upsetting the girl.

Her mother's response was a pitying look for Osmares. "Oh, dear goddesses," she whispered. "Oh, you poor—"

"Amma," said Nohana, and shook her head. "I guess you could say I've adopted her. She's my sister now, and I will take care of her."

"You've changed because of the man and woman you are now with?" asked her mother.

"That's fair to say, Amma." She lightened her tone. "How are you doing here?"

"One day after another," said her father. "It's mostly routine...well, you know that. You used to work here. But we're planning to take vacations more often, now that the night shift is able to handle the day as well. There's a nice, peaceful bay on the north coast of Lambza, and we've already had a bungalow put up there so we can stay...and who knows," he glanced at his wife, "maybe there will be another sister for you two one of these days. Or a brother."

Nohana grinned. "I guess that will make me the 'practice' child."

"Did you work here?" asked Osmares.

"Since I was about your age," Nohana told her. "I started out as the bread maid. I delivered rolls and biscuits to the booths. And butter, of course," she added quickly.

"She always forgot the butter," said her mother, to Osmares.

"Can I work here?"

Neither parent responded, but looked to Nohana.

"Why don't you and I talk about that later?" said Nohana.

"Okay. Can I have some more lemonade?"

Her father beckoned to a serving girl, who brought a fresh glass.

Nohana said, "Osmares has a good idea, though. Appa, Amma, do you need any extra help? Those women need jobs, they need...well, they need lives. It's not going to be easy, but having a job will help them in more ways than just money. I don't know whether any of them would want to work here, but if they do..."

"What do you think, Paluma?" asked her father. "She could learn on the night shift. If it works out, we might take vacations more often. I know it's another pair of hands to pay, but..."

Nohana cleared her throat for attention. "About that," she said. "We—this Unit I'm in—can pay you her wages. Or their wages. But nobody can know about it."

Her father smiled. "I understand."

"And they would need a place to stay..."

"They can have a room upstairs," said her mother. "And take meals down here. Or they can stay at the *Alloggio*." Smiling, she added, "But the food is much better here."

"I just wish I knew what it is that you're doing now, Nohana," said her father.

"Good, Appa," she said. "I'm doing good."

Osmares sat back, a tear in each eye, her hand pressed over her upper chest. "Hurts," she cried.

"You drank too fast," said Nohana. She slid a glass of water to her. "Take a sip of this, swirl it around in your mouth to warm it, then swallow slowly." The girl did so. A moment later, Nohana asked, "All better?"

"Better."

A tap at the window brought the encounter to an end. Cahill beckoned to her. The airfoils were ready for transport. Nohana raised a finger for wait a second.

"We'll be back," she told her parents. "We're not going anywhere for a while."

Hugs followed, and included Osmares.

With Osmares at her side on the bridge, Nohana swept the airfoil a kilometer out to sea. The girl's wide eyes said the experience of the ocean, and of skimming over its waves, was a first for her. She clung to the railing that ran along the instrumentation console, under the windshield, and remained steady there despite a bit of buffeting as the wind picked up.

Nohana was less than pleased with the weather. The other airfoils had at least a quarter-hour head start on her, as hers was the last to be uncrated. Forest green with black detailing, it was even color-coordinated with much of her outfits, which tended to range from pastel to deep green. It handled well against the cross-wind, and even better when she raised the altitude to three meters to avoid the spray from the agitated waves. In the distance off to starboard, lightning lit the dark clouds that were accumulating, and cast fierce shadows among them. With each flash, the girl cried out.

Nohana tokked the Palmetto on the console, raising Cahill. "Where are you?" she asked.

"About half an hour out. You?"

"This storm came up quickly. I'm not sure we can make it."

"Then don't try," he said. "Is there someplace you can lay up?"

"Any port in a storm," she said. "There's a couple fingers sticking out into the waves up ahead."

"I saw them."

"I'm going to lay up there, and hope there's shelter. Raise you when we get in there."

After she closed out, Osmares said, "I'm scared."

The wind picked up, and Nohana knew she would be unable to go further out to sea and round the tip of the closest finger. There was no choice now but to go ashore and tie up as best she could, and find an overhang that would shelter them. This area along the coast was unfamiliar to her, though the terrain was typical of the stretch, all the way past Birdrop. If they had time, they might well find such an overhang. If they had time.

"Sit down," she told Osmares. "Hold on tight to your chair, hard as you can."

With the girl as secured as possible, Nohana turned to port, riding the gusty tailwind. The course was uneven, as the winds buffeted the airfoil from side to side. She could make out the shoreline. Raindrops began to fall, a few at first, then a blinding deluge through which she could only hope she was headed in the right direction. On the instrumentation console, the altimeter bounced from one to four meters and back, and back again. She did not know whether to accelerate or slow, and did neither. Just ahead a wave crested, a large one, and the bottom of the airfoil grazed it. Fanblades spewed froth and foam, and the airfoil plowed into the water. Osmares cried out in terror, and as they spilled from the airfoil, Nohana dove toward the girl, wrapping her arms around her. Her momentum carried both of them into the turgid waters. The airfoil tumbled into them and struck Nohana on the back of her left shoulder. Lights lit up inside her head, and Osmares cried out. Nohana hung tightly onto her as they rolled with the waves.

021: Sisters

"I can't raise them," Cahill shouted. For a moment he lifted the Palmetto as if to dash it against a rock, but there were no rocks on the bridge of the *Akila*, and he brought his frustration and fear under control. "She should answer," he said, calmed by Shimmer's touch.

"I'm frightened for them, too, Pol," she said.

He caught his breath before worry put a stranglehold on it. "You'd better go aft and see to the women," he told her. "They're bound to be frightened, too."

But she was already on her way.

Cahill flopped onto the starboard captain's chair, feeling less like a captain and more like a helpless ne'er-do-well. There was *nothing* for him to do, save sit this out and find a goddess to pray to. Well, there was one thing. He could check to see whether the Palmetto actually functioned.

"Are you all right, Pol?" Ayvy asked, when he raised her.

"Yeah. No."

"I can come over."

"No."

"Pol, it's only ten meters."

"No!"

"You *do* have your clothes on?"

The incongruency made him laugh, and more annoyed with himself and his inaction. "Ayvy, don't. Just...don't."

"She'll be all right," Ayvy soothed. "This is her world, after all."

"This is not your common storm here. Ayvy, I gotta...gotta...in case she toks."

"Understood. You know where I am."

Yeah, he thought, closing out. But I don't know where *she*...where *they* is. Are. Movement at his side brought his head around. Shimmer stood there, holding two mugs of hot cocoa.

"Best thing in a storm," she said sagely, and handed him one. With a glance at the port chair, she asked, "May I sit there?"

"Oh, Shimmer, of course you can. And thank you."

She did so. "Mind that marshmallow mustache." Suddenly she leaped to her feet and pointed at the Videx, almost sloshing her cocoa. "Look! Look!"

Just at the horizon, the storm clouds were breaking. There, the sky was clear, and lit by sunlight.

"It's moving off," she said, though the rain continued to pound the 'skip. "It's almost over."

"Another hour yet," Cahill groused, frustrated again.

"Maybe sooner." She surveyed him, trying to find a way to ease his worries. "At least we secured the other airfoils."

He whirled on her. "You think that matters to me?" he snapped.

She threw her hands up defensively. "No, no, I'm just saying..." She stopped, not knowing what it was, exactly, she was saying. She backed away a couple steps, then turned and fled aft toward the spare stateroom.

Lips bloodless with irritation at himself, Cahill smacked his fist on the console. After giving her a few minutes, he went to knock on the stateroom door. She took several seconds to respond, but at least it was not a demand for him to go away. He slid the door open cautiously and stood just outside.

"I'm sorry," he said quietly, but with resolve. "I'm worried and frightened. I know you are, too."

For a long time Shimmer sat on the berth and regarded him. Presently she lifted the tip of her index finger across her upper lip. "You missed some marshmallow," she said.

He tried with his tongue and missed, then used his sleeve. Shimmer got up and approached him. He did not expect the hug she gave him. He held her, and whispered his apology once more. She nodded against his chest before easing away.

Across the emotions, their eyes met. "You are my friend, my companion, and my partner," he told her. "I'm glad you're a part of us. I'll try not to growl at you."

"I'll try to be more understanding."

He drew her toward the doorway. "Let's go see if the storm is abating."

***

Woozy, Nohana struggled both to stay afloat and hold onto Osmares. Between waves, she could just touch the tips of her toes to the bottom while her mouth was at the water level. But the waves were rolling the capsized airfoil without regard to direction or attitude, and another great wave drove it toward them. Already her left shoulder was almost useless, the muscles in her upper arm slack and unresponsive. She felt as if she should be bleeding. Her head ached as well, for the airfoil had caught her a glancing blow in passing.

When the wave broke, there was only one thing for them to do. "We're going under," Nohana yelled into her ear. "Take a deep breath, and stay with me."

They reached the mud and muck on the sea bottom. Nohana held them there as long as she dared. She was good for over two minutes even in turbulent water, but the girl enveloped in her right arm had never been in an ocean. She wished she could see the airfoil. It would be disastrous if they rose just as it was bearing down on them.

Osmares's hand tore at Nohana's clothing. Now she had no choice but to bring them back up. As their heads broke the surface of the water, the airfoil loomed over them. The aft deck collapsed on top of them and shoved them back down into the mud. Stuck itself, the airfoil held them in place. Nohana found a pocket of air trapped against the aft deck, and pushed Osmares's face into it, willing her to breathe. Only one face would fit; Nohana's lungs screamed for air.

The next wave carried the airfoil forward, and the stern taffrail struck the back of Nohana's head in passing. Dazed, she could only stumble along the mud. In shallower waters now, she breathed and choked and coughed, and she had no idea where she was. Her right hand vised the girl's forearm as she staggered alongside. Only the fading luminescence of the waves lit their way; the lightning had abated. The sand of the beach came into focus, and went out again. Nohana's head throbbed with each step she took. She had stopped caring where she was now; only the girl mattered.

A wave broke behind them and carried them toward shore. Chest-deep, then hip-deep, and they were able to wade clumsily. Unnoticed, rain kept them drenched. Wet sand made their feet slip, and they both fell to their knees as the next wave died around them. Nohana spilled forward, and foam filled her nose. She drew a breath through her mouth, and spat sand. Sprawled beside her, the girl spat as well.

"C'mon," gasped Osmares, on hands and knees now. Rain washed her hair over her eyes, and she plucked it away angrily. She tugged at Nohana's arm, to no avail.

Nohana's head swam. She was dimly aware that she was on the verge of passing out, with waves still bound for her. Feeling had returned to her left arm, but she was still unable to use it.

Osmares was standing now. She yanked at Nohana's arm, and grabbed her by the hair. "Come *on!*" she screamed, and fell down from the effort she was making. Another wave died around them. Water flew into Nohana's nose and mouth. She sputtered, and coughed.

"You have to move!" cried Osmares.

Nohana rose to her hands and knees, but her left arm collapsed when she put weight on it. The girl's fingers were tangled in her wet hair. Through blurred vision Nohana just made out a great mass of rock. A bit of light behind them brought it into focus—one of the fingers that punched the ocean.

With a great final effort Nohana rose to her feet and staggered toward the rock. Osmares held her up now. They reached the lighter sand beyond the high-water mark. Out to sea, the horizon lightened. Nohana's vision remained blurred.

"Here," said the girl. "Under here."

Nohana looked up. A shelf of rock protruded over them, blocking some of the rain.

"Hold onto me," cried Osmares. "Sit, sit. Sit here. I'm right here."

Nohana collapsed onto the sand, and rolled to sit up. She drew her legs up and wrapped her right arm around them. Her left arm flopped into place above the right, and poised there. Her right hand grasped it to hold it in place.

"Your shoulder," fretted Osmares.

"Think...dislo...dislocated," said Nohana. Her vision was clearing, but the ache in her head remained. "Where...?"

"Palmetto?" asked Osmares.

Mentally Nohana examined her pockets. "Left front," she said, her breathing shallow and rapid. "Can't...get out."

The girl fumbled for it, and slipped it free. She laid it on her leg so Nohana could tok it. As soon as her right hand moved, her left fell onto the sand. Blinking, she tokked the device.

Nothing happened.

"What's wrong?" cried Osmares. "Why won't they answer?"

"Don't know. Broken. Wet." She steadied herself with a longer breath. Her shoulder ached now, enough to make her forget her head.

"What can I do?" Osmares pleaded. Tentatively she reached out toward Nohana's shoulder, but was reluctant to touch it.

"Nothing you can do," said Nohana. "Medic...pop back in."

"But it's hurting you."

The wind picked up, as the back end of the storm began to pass. The rain diminished to a few drops, then picked up again, and slowed once more. Water trickled from the overhang, but they were well under it. Light made them blink. Within moments the sun would be shining.

"What are we going to do?" Osmares asked.

Nohana started to shake her head, and thought better of it. "They'll find..."

Osmares reached for Nohana's left hand, and in doing so, their heads collided. After all that had happened, this was enough. Nohana spilled sideways, unconscious.

022: The Fitting Room

Nohana awoke to bright lights and cracked lips. She knew she was in the clinic, but had no idea how she had come to be there. She sensed, rather than saw, that she was not alone. Her head felt turbaned. Her left arm refused to move, confined as it was to an immobilizing sling. A dull ache had set up house in her shoulder and was moving furniture around. She recalled throbbing in her head, but that seemed to have subsided now. To her left, the window invited sunlight. She turned her head to the right.

Shimmer and Osmares were sitting at a makeshift table, playing some incomprehensible game with dice that made the girl laugh. Both stopped the game when she moved, and the dice tumbled to the floor. Tears welled in Osmares's dark eyes as she moved to the bed and threw her arms around Nohana.

Right behind her came Shimmer. "Oh, Doctor Genevieve said it could be any time," she sobbed. "A day, a month. You were comatose, you...oh, goddesses, Nohana, I missed you."

Nohana found her throat too dry for her to speak. She managed a, "Water?"

Shimmer shook her head. "Just a little, until the doctor sees you."

"I'll get her," said Osmares, and dashed off.

Shimmer held her cup of water while Nohana took several sips, the first of which descended like a hard lump into her stomach. Coughing, she nudged Shimmer's hand away.

"How...long?" she gasped.

"Six days."

"But...but I was...supposed...supposed to help, help them, I..."

"It's all done," said Shimmer. She looked as if she wanted to sit down on the edge of the bed, but there was no room for her. Drawing the chair up and crossing her arms on the pad for support served almost as well. "The prefabs, the wells, the furniture, everything. And I have oils and canvas and pads...and...I've been drawing...I have a painting working now... Nohana, I missed you."

"I love you, too."

Nohana tried to sit up, but Shimmer gently pressed her chest to push her back down. "Not until the doctor," she admonished. "I don't want anything to delay your recovery."

Doctor Genevieve entered the room with her Palmetto in hand, her eyes on Nohana. "Are you ready to go home?" she asked.

Nohana blinked. "I-I can?"

"As soon as you will be disconnected. But I should you apprise your condition. A moment. Your eyes open, please." She shone a light into each of Nohana's eyes in turn, and made little sounds of satisfaction. "Yes, good, your response of pupils is good. No concussion. You have head bruise, it will heal. Your shoulder healed, the sling is not you need now. My aide of nurse will take it off, and remove the feeds." Genevieve's sepia eyes studied her. "Do you have questions?"

"My shoulder is okay?" asked Nohana.

"You may know stiffness and very minor ache for few days. Nothing more." She flashed a broad smile of ivory teeth. "You were good patient. Not talk too much."

The woman who came in to remove Nohana's sling and feeds looked familiar, and it took only a few seconds to recognize her as one of the three women Doctor Genevieve had taken from the beach with her for more intense medical treatment. She was attired in medical greens, with a name tag of white block letters on a black background affixed to her tunic. It read MAFALDA. Shimmer had already reacquainted herself, but kept out of her way while she worked. Mafalda walked with a limp, her right leg in an isocast that protected the ankle, but she was agile enough to round the bed and back. Nohana felt little stings as the feeds were withdrawn from her right arm and hand, but her left arm felt mobile enough after the sling was removed.

"I brought you some fresh clothing," said Shimmer. She indicated a bound bundle on the table under the window.

Nohana took both of Osmares's hands in hers. "I think you saved my life," she told the girl. "It's all vague now, but I think I remember that."

"You saved mine," Osmares replied.

"I think you deserve some ice cream."

"What is ice cream?"

Nohana dressed cautiously, still feeling her way around her recovery. Her left arm and shoulder issued a couple of feeble protests, but otherwise performed as she expected. At the window, tugging her jersey down, she paused to gaze out at Bassoon. She could see all the way to the ocean, to the docks and airfoils and fishing vessels. The ocean greeted her calmly, as if to beg forgiveness.

Shimmer made a little gesture for attention. "Someone wants to see you," she said, without enthusiasm.

"Where are Pol and Ayvy?" she asked.

Shimmer did not answer, but turned and left the room, a jerk of her head indicating that Nohana should follow. As before, Osmares stayed by her side. Shimmer led them to a room with a closed door, and knocked on it. A uniformed constable opened it, looked at Nohana, and bade her and the others enter.

Damon Faben lay on the bed, feeds in his left arm, the top sheet and a quilt tucked over his chest and under his arms. His pale face bore no expression as his eyes took her in. She drew to within a pace of the bed, while Osmares stood behind her and Shimmer waited outside. The guard watched them closely while pretending not to.

Annoyed by the silence, Nohana considered leaving. It was up to him to speak. But she had other matters on her mind; he occupied but a mote of her attention. "What did you want, Damon?" she said.

Their eyes met, and for long seconds he did not respond. Finally, he looked at the window. "I-I didn't think you'd come."

"If I had known where I was going, I probably wouldn't have. One last time, Damon. What did you want?"

"I don't," he tried, and swallowed. "Don't know, now. You've...changed."

"Have you?" He did not answer her. "I'll tell you what," she said. "I'll make this simple. Regardless of what you say or do, I'm not coming back to you, not ever. Not just because of what you did to Shimmer, or wanted to do to me, but because I am where I am supposed to be and doing what I am supposed to be doing and with the people I am supposed to be with. Let me make it even clearer: if you come after me or my people again, whether as yourself or by means of a proxy, I won't leave enough of you to cremate.

"Now, having said that. Damon, you've made bad choices and you've suffered the consequences, as is fitting. If you're looking for fault, try the mirror. If you move toward a life where you make good decisions and earn positive consequences, I will cheer for you and applaud you. You're still alive, so you have the abilities and the possibilities. It's your choice whether you avail yourself of them. I can even tell you where you should start this new journey. Go see Victrail Leos."

"He's a life coach."

"Yeah. You need coaching."

"But...he costs money."

"There are jobs down on the docks," Nohana told him. "After you get out of here, go find one."

"That's scut labor," he said bitterly. "Besides, I'll be in jail."

She shook her head. "Not on my account." She drew a long breath. "Damon, I'm not going to file charges, and neither will Ayvy or Shimmer. What the Constabulary does is up to them, of course. I've already told you what will happen if you come after me or mine again. Now, this is my personal attitude and opinion, but work on the docks is better than living off your parents' money.

"But you do what you will, Damon. You can have a better life, and do something with it, or not. You can even have no life at all. You are the one who has to choose."

Without waiting for a response, she turned around and marched out the door, holding Osmares's hand as they departed.

Shimmer joined them. "He makes me want to bathe," she said.

"I know the feeling."

023: Paper Chase

If only one Fringe world was immune from Confederation attack or interference, it was Relay. Originally settled by a silver mining concern that gradually expanded into platinum and iridium, Relay soon became a way-station for travel from the Confederation to and from the Fringes. A century later, commerce and civilian travel was interrupted by a war neither side could win, but which ended with the guerrilla threat to the corporations of the Confederation. When there's no money in it, nobody fights wars against those who seek the freedom to be left alone.

Bankers and financial investment houses, taking advantage of minimal legal obstructions, soon thereafter flocked to Relay, where they established a central district surrounded by dwellings and smaller enterprises. This city, too, was called Relay, and grew to be the only settlement of significant size. Mining and smelting continued, and ingots of valuable metals were stored in the Bank of Relay as proof against further attack—the idea being that in the event of Confederation interference of any kind, these precious metals would be dumped onto the Confederation markets, devaluing and debasing the currency already in use there. Corporations fear impoverishment above all else; they left the Fringes alone.

With banking unregulated and secure, all manner of clients dealt on Relay—including some whose finances were stolen or otherwise of questionable origin. Whatever was kept in the Bank of Relay was safe until the end of time. Eventually, even the corporations saw the benefits of preventing tax assessors from viewing their financial records, and moved their monies to Relay—which treated them like any other individuals with ill-gotten gains; in other words, with the respect that was warranted by the amount of the deposit.

Although Ayvy had lived in and around a major corporation for most of her first eighteen years, she had never seen buildings like those on Relay. Tall, immaculate, and radiant in the silver-white star that held the world in thrall, the structures were easily large enough to hold all the corporate proceeds and much, much more. Her neck ached, looking up. Cahill, who was carrying a cold drink, pressed it to the back of her head and neck, and gave her some relief. She sipped at her own drink while they passed along the walkways—called boardwalks here, although they were made of plasticrete—and checked out the merchandise in the windows of the small shops and the kiosks.

"I suppose you've been here before," she said to him, as she peered in at racks and shelves of silversmith craftwork.

"Twice," he replied. "One was a fool's errand, obvious from the outset. The lowest accounts clerks won't disclose their own names without an Act of Parliament...if there was a Parliament. Even then...well, so I returned to ConSec with a negative report, and the case was filed under unsolvable."

"That must have been frustrating."

Cahill shrugged. "All part of the job."

"And the second time?"

"Actually, that was the second time. The first, I had to tell a middle management supervisor that his son had... been killed. I was to gauge his reaction, because it was just possible the man had been instrumental in the death."

"Was he?"

He shook his head. "No. And that made it more difficult for both of us." He pointed at an ornate silver salt cellar on a display shelf. "I wouldn't mind having one of those."

"And only six thousand thalers," she said sardonically. "This item is priced to move!"

"Compared to platinum, iridium, and palladium, silver isn't worth much," he said, as they moved on toward the next intersection. "But the lost art of silversmithing has been reborn here. The work is exquisite. That cellar will one day adorn some plutocrat's dinner table during a soirée."

They waited at the intersection while airfoils crossed it in either direction. When the signal changed, they walked toward the Safe Deposit Repository—at an above-ground height of ten levels one of the shorter buildings, this one of off-white cut stone with royal purple trim. The guard post before the front door was manned by a tall young woman in a pastel lilac uniform, who carefully checked the identification of two individuals while Ayvy and Cahill approached. Her name tag read Eila Wanheinan, and under that, Sergeant. Her smile appeared to have been sewed onto her mouth, but her violet eyes were intense and alert. After a very brief inspection Ayvy determined that the eye color was due to tinted lenses.

Ayvy's heart was a bird trapped in a cage as she passed the guard her real identification and stood still while the fac-rec matched the face to the card. Earlier she had considered the possibility that the Bank of Relay had received negative instructions regarding her, but now she was confronted with the reality. After the guard merely scrutinized the card and ran it through the validation slot, she passed it back with a cursory, "Thank you," and Ayvy resisted the idea of breathing a sigh of relief. Instead, she simply accepted the acknowledgement as her due.

Cahill came next, and now Ayvy held her breath. She did not need him to access her safe deposit box, or to accompany her into and back out of the Repository, or for any other reason once they were inside. But she wanted him there. On impatient feet she waited. To clear him took several seconds longer, but in the end the guard returned his card, and together they marched inside toward the check-in counter.

"I think we're being set up," he whispered.

Ayvy skidded to a stop. "What? Here?"

"Keep your voice down, Ayvy. Just go along with it. We're not under threat, not here, but I think our progress is being monitored through me. That process at the guard shack took a good ten seconds longer than it should have done."

"Oh, goddesses..."

"Yeah. Act natural, and let's do what we came to do."

At the counter, Ayvy relaxed a little, even though this was the critical moment of their visit. She could ill afford to appear nervous in any way. Her hand shook just once as she slid her card across the counter and again allowed fac-rec to operate.

The clerk was an innocuous young man who would not stand out in even a small crowd. He wore no name tag, only a standard banking-gray outsuit. Unlike the guard outside, his eyes were the color of fresh water.

"And how may I help you this day, *M'selle* Vigdisdottir?"

Ayvy relaxed more at the sound of her name. Earlier, she and Cahill had discussed under which name her father might have arranged the box, and concluded that he would have used her chosen name to help conceal his involvement.

"My companion and I would like to be escorted to my safe deposit box to examine the contents," she said.

"In that case, I'll need to verify his identity as well, *M'selle*."

"But it's not his box, it's mine."

"Nevertheless, *M'selle*—"

"Oh, very well," she said, with feigned exasperation.

She edged aside while Cahill went through the process as well. Again there was a delay of a few seconds, but his identity was confirmed. The clerk beckoned to an escort, a young woman whose yellow outsuit blended well with her hair. She made a little gesture for them to follow her, but did nothing to invite conversation. Her very silence was now part of the process: what transpired now was and could be of no interest to her.

They entered a secure lift—the escort had to show her eye to a retinal scan in order to open the doors. Once inside, the doors closed automatically; Cahill glanced up at the little sensor that could only be seen by someone who knew to look for it. Security was monitoring the descent; three people were authorized to take the lift, and three people were now aboard it. The escort keyed for the level designated as B7, which meant the seventh level underground. Ayvy felt her stomach float, then settle back down. After only seconds the lift slowed and stopped. Her knees bent. The door opened.

The escort beckoned. Light echoes followed them as she led them along a hallway of doors, whose close spacing indicated small rooms. Above each door was the numeral seven, followed by successive three-digit numbers starting at zero zero one, odd numbers on the left, evens on the right. After perhaps thirty meters the escort reached 7-016. At her touch to the pad on the wall, the door opened.

"When you are finished," she said to Ayvy, in a voice like an automaton, "simply summon the lift and keep your face clearly visible as you enter. The lift will take you directly to the lobby." She did not wait for an acknowledgement, but returned the way she had brought them.

Ayvy glanced through the open doorway. The room, two meters wide and five deep, looked sterile. Every surface, even the counter that ran across the back wall, was matte white. On the floor in front of the counter stood a white plastic chair contoured for comfort. As Ayvy entered, a rectangular door lifted in the back wall and a flat box of gray structural plastic was deposited onto the counter.

Cahill closed the door behind them. There was no way to secure it from the inside, but it could not now be opened from the outside. Slowly they approached the counter and the box.

"I think," said Ayvy, swallowing hard, "I had better sit down."

"Would you like me to open it?" he asked.

"If you would, Pol." She thought for a moment, and added, "If you can."

"Anyone can, as long as they're authorized to be in this room."

While Ayvy tensed, watching, he undid the latch and lifted the lid, pushing it back to rest against the wall. "A paper case," she breathed. "Nohana was right."

Cahill lifted it out and set it on the counter. It measured about fifty by thirty centimeters by ten centimeters deep, with a black carrying handle on one side. A simple latch secured the lid.

Ayvy peered into the safe deposit box; the paper case had been the only item in it. She drew a breath to steady herself. "All right, let's see what the fuss is all about."

Cahill reluctantly shook his head. "I think we'd better just take it and leave," he said. "We can open it in null-space."

"And...the deposit box?"

He pointed to instructions printed on the top of the counter. "Push the box back through that door. The door will close, and a conveyor belt will return it automatically to its storage place."

"Which is where?"

"Deep within the bowels of the bank. Ready?"

She lifted the case. Startled by its lightness, she almost hit herself with it. "It feels almost empty," she said.

"Then that's going to disappoint a lot of people. Come, let's get out of here."

They gained the lobby without incident. No one accosted them as they made their way to the main door. The guard gave them a cursory nod as they stepped outside. When they reached the intersection they had to cross, Cahill's Palmetto signaled.

At his tok, the face of a rather agitated young man appeared. "*M'sieur* Cahill?" he asked breathlessly, but did not wait for a response. "A representative from Confederation Resources urgently needs you to wait for him on Relay to discuss certain security matters."

"I understand," Cahill said amiably. "We can meet in one hour at a patio table at *Passengers Restaurant* in the Spaceport Terminal. Who shall I look for?"

"I-I-I don't know. I was instructed to relay this message."

"No pun intended, I suppose."

"*M'sieur?*"

"Never mind. I'm wearing a black outsuit. He can't help but spot me at a white table."

The young man gushed. "Oh, thank you, thank you. It's...this is my job, you know."

"And you do it so well. One hour, then," he finished, and closed out.

"Conigli?" asked Ayvy, as he put away the device.

"I wouldn't think so. This is still the Fringes, after all. No, this is probably someone on his personal security staff, and Conigli is holding his family or someone close to him as proof against failure."

"That's grotesque."

"Yeah."

He flagged down an airfoil-for-hire and gave the pilot instructions. Ayvy's knuckles whitened around the case handle as she sat down on the port bench. She rested the case on her lap and felt weak, almost on the verge of fainting. Cahill's arm around her shoulders kept her upright.

"Almost there," he told her. "Relax."

"I can't. I can't relax. It's...oh, I don't know..." She turned her face to him. "Pol, we're not actually going... going to that restaurant, are we?"

"Of course not. I left my black outsuit on Cullen's Lode."

She gave a feeble laugh. "You're impossible."

"Merely improbable."

The spires of the main terminal came into view as they rounded a bend in the glideway. The sight of safety made Ayvy worry all the more. They were approaching the critical moment. As they passed a park, they saw the rest of the Spaceport. Cahill tapped on the back of the pilot's seat.

"This is good here," Cahill told him.

The airfoil slowed. "You sure?"

Cahill handed him a bit of folding money, with the number 100 in clear view. "Quite sure," he said. "And thanks."

The airfoil stopped at the edge of the park, and he and Ayvy climbed down. After it flew away, he looked around the park, and seeing that they were alone, he tokked his Palmetto. Two seconds later, the *Akila* appeared on the grass before them. After a dash up the ramp and through the hatchway, and a sharp command from Cahill, they were in null-space.

And safe.

024: All Good Things

Melting ice cream dribbled down the front of Osmares's shirt as she stood on the bridge of the airfoil. Wind blew her hair, and now and then a bit of spray moistened her face. Nohana thought the girl looked happy. She herself, however, was less than pleased.

Still incredulous, she asked Shimmer once more. "They went to Relay by themselves?"

"They had to go," said Shimmer. "According to Cah...Pol, a mess was developing in the Confederation. Secret meetings, and rumors of secret meetings. And nobody knows what's going on. Pol said we needed to identify the danger. So he and Ayvy had to go."

"Without us," Nohana said dully. "Without you and me."

"Someone needed to watch over you while you were...asleep," said Shimmer.

"You."

"And me," added Osmares.

"I'm the victim of a conspiracy," Nohana shouted to the ocean. But she was laughing. "Okay, I understand," she said, sobering. "Now tell me why we can't raise them."

"Pol said not to," Shimmer told her, as if it explained everything. "Anyway, he said they'd be back later today."

Osmares finished her ice cream, and lifted the hem of her shirt to wipe her mouth. "I like the ocean," she said, looking out to port.

"We'll take a walk," said Nohana. "Maybe find some shells." She rested her hand on Shimmer's shoulder. "I haven't asked about you," she said. "I'm sorry."

"I sold a painting," Shimmer said brightly.

"Oh, tell me!"

"While you were sleeping, I did one of you," she said, and called it up on her Palmetto.

Nohana saw herself in a shadowed room with the sunlight coming from the left through a lacy curtained window to illuminate a table, on which rested a tea service. She was pouring for two. She was wearing a white summer dress, translucent where the sunlight struck it. The table was of some dark wood, and covered with a lace-trimmed white cloth. Two chairs waited at the ready. A set of shelves of the same dark wood stood against the wall at the right side of the painting. On one of the shelves squatted an antique clock, with the minute hand just shy of the next hour. In the painting, Nohana had one eye on that clock, as if in anticipation of someone's arrival.

"It's beautiful," she sighed. "Oh, Shimmer, this is… is…wait. You sold this? To whom?"

"Your parents." She grinned. "I cheated a little on the sale. I painted it for them. I knew they would like it."

"A sale is a sale."

"Yeah. My first."

"Not your last," Nohana said with utter certainty. "Where is it hanging?"

"In the front room of their house, I think they said. Certainly not in the tavern, where it can get greasy and… well, you know."

"It sounds like I have to pay them a visit."

"I think you should."

"Are we there yet?" asked Osmares.

Nohana glanced at the shoreline. "Birdrop coming up," she told the girl. "So about fifteen more minutes."

The girl looked out to sea. The blue sky reflected in her eyes. "No storms," she said softly.

"Are you worried?" Nohana asked.

Osmares shivered, but did not respond.

"It's just weather," Shimmer told her. "We'll be more careful."

Osmares leaned against Nohana. "I don't want anything to happen to you."

"Or to you," she said, and tousled the girl's hair. She turned a little to port, to swing her around a cape. "But sometimes storms on this section of the coast can creep up on you. We just have to stay vigilant."

"Do you think lightning will strike the sand again?"

The question brought a puzzled frown to Nohana's brow. "I suppose so. Why would you ask that?"

"That thing we dug out of the sand was from lightning," said Osmares.

"We looked it up," said Shimmer. "It's called fulgurite. Lightning fuses sand into odd shapes. Some of them are larger than this airfoil."

"And I sold this one," added Osmares.

"You did?"

"A man gave me five hundred thalers for it."

Nohana had a pained look. "But...but that was something special to you."

"If there are storms, I can find more."

"Or maybe make more," said Shimmer.

"I don't see how," said Nohana.

"It's simple," Shimmer told her. "We stick lightning rods in the sand. Lightning strikes them, fuses the sand, and we dig up the results."

Nohana swung the airfoil back to starboard, and aimed it inland. They swept over grass and between trees, and finally the *Black Ice* came into view, followed by the prefab house, all assembled. Absorbed by the sight of home, she brought the airfoil to hover twenty meters away. Slowly she docked it. Her eyes wavered from the house. Her mouth hung open, and her lips quivered with the pounding of her heart.

"They did it," she said, half gasp and half sigh.

"*We* did it," said Shimmer.

Nohana disembarked, then helped Osmares get down. Together the three stepped slowly toward the house, and the flagstone walkway that led to the front door.

"It's larger than I had imagined," said Nohana.

"That's the extra two rooms," Shimmer told her.

Nohana could only stare at her, puzzled.

"I...I decided I didn't want to live alone," Shimmer explained. "I talked it over with Ayvy and Pol, and they... they changed the prefab order. One room is for sleeping. The other is for my art, my painting. I had a special ventilation system installed in it. But I'll do most of my oils and acrylics outside. I'll keep my rooms clean," she added quickly. "And I'll cook meals, and—"

Nohana's hand over her mouth stopped her. "Dock it back down," she said. "Who told you to cook?"

"Nobody. I just thought..." Sadness flushed her face. "Don't...don't you want me to live with..."

"Oh, Shimmer, of course I do. I just didn't expect..."

"Well...you *have* been asleep."

"I have a room, too," Osmares said brightly. "Do you want to see?"

A puff of displaced air stopped Nohana's response. She turned to look at the *Akila*, just arrived. "At least they're back," she breathed.

The hatch opened, the ramp extruded. Cahill and Ayvy trudged down the incline. Their faces were as grave as Nohana had ever seen them. They appeared to be in the mood for beverages far stronger than coffee. Cahill toted a paper case in his left hand, while Ayvy was carrying a small canvas bag.

"What is it?" Nohana cried, hurrying to them. "What's wrong, what's happened?"

"We have to be ready to leave at a moment's notice," Cahill told her. "If we get even that much notice."

She looked from one to the other. "I-I don't understand..."

Ayvy held up the paper case. "Let's go inside," she said. "We'll explain, and then we'll pack a few things."

"Pack?" fretted Nohana. "What are you saying? What's *happened*?"

But Cahill and Ayvy passed her, and continued to the front door of the house.

025: End Game

The five gathered around the dining table. Only Osmares sat down; the others, in various moods, could only stand around. After assessing their expressions, Shimmer took crystal tumblers from the cupboard and opened a new bottle of Ardbeg, pouring whiskey even for Osmares. Cahill took only a polite sip, as if he meant to remain sober.

He did not signal for attention. He simply began speaking, in a desolated voice.

"The paper case contained a detached drive," he told them. "That drive contains files and documents Colin McKey meant to use against most of the other corporations in order to aggrandize himself and his corporate distilleries. Although we cannot know for certain now, it appears likely that he was waiting for the optimal moment to spring it on the corporate Chairs. He must have alluded to some of the information on the drive, because Chair Conigli was aware of it. Although he knew very little, it was enough to instill fear into him, not an easy task to accomplish."

He paused for a quick glance at Ayvy. "We suspect that Conigli, aware of the probable contents of these files, meant to use them himself after McKey's death, and to the same end. What he did not want—what the Chairs and hierarchs absolutely do not want—is public exposure of the contents. Broadly speaking, the corporations do not fear the so-called masses, who are not known to band together for a life-or-death cause. What they do fear is a mass and spontaneous uprising against themselves and their estates and their properties. I, we, understand that fear. The resultant disruption could well kill billions, of starvation, fighting, burning...

"And that uprising will definitely occur if there is exposure. You see, we have all been lied to, from the first day we entered Confederation Schools. Yes, we all knew that a certain small amount of enslavement had accompanied the expansion of humanity to the worlds of this section of the Spiral Arm. In retrospect, it was—given the proclivities of corporations—inevitable. There has always been a virulent demand for the cheapest possible labor. While we abhorred that part of our history, we accepted it. After all, it was in the past, and each minute of each day took us further away from those dark times.

"What happened was this: the first entities to take advantage of the development of Track, of faster-than-light travel, were the corporations of old Earth. There were worlds to exploit and develop, to grow rich and fat off. There was untold wealth just waiting to be accumulated. But there was a problem: corporate executives do not do manual labor. They do not do the sort of work necessary to develop a resource or a world. They hire others to do that work, and to do it at the lowest possible labor costs. An additional problem was that relatively few people wanted to find opportunities and establish careers on other worlds. They preferred the security of the familiar, however awful it might be. Those few who did leave Earth were adventurers looking for easy wealth—gold, gems, and so forth; or they were seeking new lives away from Earth and the corporations. Most of humanity, however, remained home.

"What to do?

"The corporations resorted to the historically easiest solution. They enslaved people and sent them to worlds to exploit those resources. Work or die. The process of human trafficking was relatively simple, and was enabled by Track. A schooner-class spacecraft downdocks at the edge of a village; corporate security forces emerge and force as many villagers as possible in five minutes' time onto the craft. As a demonstration of their power, the forces often killed five people or so arbitrarily, outright. This process was eminently successful because no Earth security force could possibly respond to this stealthy incursion in five minutes. Fifty minutes, maybe, but not five."

"That's where the term 'Swoopies' comes from," Nohana broke in, as she made a connection. "The corporate craft swooped in and scooped up the workers it needed."

Cahill nodded. "And as the corporations grew, they needed more and more workers...slaves. At first, the manufactured items on other worlds were exported to Earth for sale. But the more slaves there were on other worlds, the more settlements arose. Those slaves needed to buy food, clothing, shelter, entertainment, knives, forks and spoons, too. So while they were paid...and paid a pittance...they returned through their purchases much of the money to the corporations that had enslaved them. Eventually, over time, most of the original slaves—or more precisely, their descendants—gained freedom to some extent, though not completely. They wanted improved wages and working conditions. In this way, they became 'spoiled' goods, tainted 'assets.' Rather than improve their lot, the corporations simply left them to live or die on their own. A kind of armistice developed, in which former slaves developed small businesses, which grew into larger businesses, which eventually competed with the corporations and were soon absorbed by them. But in an infinity of untapped resources and worlds, there was always a need for more and more slaves.

"Swooping never actually stopped. It continues to this day, in one form or another. And not just on Earth. As the Confederation expands to other worlds, it Swoops people from worlds already settled and moves them to where the work is, as Ayvy and Shimmer discovered recently. That human trafficking," he held up the detached drive, "is what's recorded here. As much of it as McKey could get his hands on, and I'd say he got most of it. And this information will come as a hard shock to people who have long assumed that they are now relatively free.

"Here's how I think it will happen. Once people learn of all this, they will go after the Chairs, the hierarchs, the estates...*and* the colluders. They will kill as many of them as they can. Many insurgents will also die in the process. Those who have power never, ever give it up willingly, and absolutely never give up absolute power.

They'll fight to keep what they have, and to teach the insurgents a lesson.

"This is the history of humanity that they don't dare teach in Confederation Schools." He looked at Nohana. "I daresay they don't even teach much of it out here in the Fringes."

"Some," she said. "But as you pointed out, it's treated as a thing of the past."

"Yes. Now, the Confederation fears the Fringe worlds. About 400 years ago, a war was fought between the two, without a decision. This, even though the forces of the Confederation were vastly superior. But the Fringe worlds were and are populated by dissidents, by those who were able to flee from the corporate worlds and corporate-created societies and develop on their own. By those who will fight back, whatever the cost."

Cahill took a deep breath. Having come to the end of the history, he now had to produce his conclusion.

"The Confederation has no choice," he said, in the tone of an epitaph. "It cannot allow these documents to become public knowledge. They will find a way to come for us without provoking a new war with the Fringe worlds."

"Why can't we just give them the drive?" Shimmer asked.

"Oh, we can," said Ayvy, speaking up for the first time. "But we're dealing with corporations. Because they are dishonest, they assume everyone else is also dishonest. In this case, they'll assume we made copies. We can't disseminate this information if we are dead."

"What if we make copies and give them to others, to be publicized in the event of our deaths?" asked Nohana.

Cahill pursed his lips, thinking. "That might work," he conceded. "But it could also get a lot of innocent people killed. Much depends on the lengths the Confederation will go to suppress these files. And we have no way of knowing what that is."

"Then we take preemptive action," said Nohana. "We kill the hierarchs first, before they come for us."

Cahill shook his head. "We might get one or two, or even three, before they realize what's happening. At that point, security will tighten unbelievably around them... we'd never get through. Which would put us back where we started."

"So we keep moving," Shimmer said dully.

"They don't know about you," Ayvy told her. "Or about Osmares. And very likely not about you, Nohana."

Nohana licked her lips. Her voice shook. "What... what are you saying?"

Neither Ayvy nor Cahill answered.

"No!" Nohana took a step back. A burst of tears flooded her eyes, and blood drained from her face. "Oh, no! Oh, goddesses, no! You *can't do* this to us!"

Aside from distraught expressions, there was still no response.

Nohana palmed tears away, but still they continued in a cloudburst. Her heart felt hollow. It was still pumping, but nothing was flowing inside her. Her head swam and her knees buckled, but somewhere she found the strength and the will to remain upright.

"What...whatever hap...happened to talking things over?" she asked. "Discussing things? What happened to that?"

"That was for when the Unit faced danger," Ayvy said placatingly. "This is different."

"H-how?" sobbed Nohana. Then she shrieked it. "*How?* What's a Unit if not a Unit? How?"

"Nohana," Shimmer said softly.

Her arm went around Nohana's shoulders. Nohana wanted to shrug herself free, but could not summon the desire to do so.

"How?" she asked once more.

"Because you are in danger," Ayvy told her pointedly. "You and Shimmer and Osmares and my mother. And we, Pol and I, *are the danger*. We have to go. You have to stay."

"Take us with you," Nohana pleaded.

Cahill shook his head. "That will not reduce the danger to you. I know you understand this, Nohana," he went on, his tone begging her for that understanding. His eyes moistened. "I know in time you'll see it has to be this way."

"In *time*?" she screamed. "How-how-how...how *long*?" She clapped tear-wet hands over her ears. "Don't say forever. I can't hear you say forever. Don't you dare say it."

"We'll work something out," said Cahill. "We will. But in the meantime, you all have to be safe. Ayvy?"

"Please, pay attention," said Ayvy. She raised the little canvas bag. "In here is a new fundscard. You now have two billion thalers to work with. Continue the Unit's work, but do so quietly. Don't draw attention to yourselves. There's also a special Palmetto in here, courtesy of Confederation Security and Pol. Untraceable, and the transmissions are undetectable. Palm us on it now and then. And we'll Palm you on it to keep you posted."

Nohana refused to accept it. If she didn't accept it, they couldn't leave.

Ayvy laid the bag on the table. Nohana's heart broke.

"We're taking the *Akila*," said Ayvy, while Cahill went to the back rooms. "You'll use the *Black Ice* whenever you need it. It has a different identity and transponder. Freya will explain it to you."

Nohana nodded; even that little movement took an effort.

Cahill returned with two travel bags. "We're going to see Vigdis now, and then we'll..." His throat tightened. He could not speak.

Nohana nodded.

Ayvy swallowed hard. "Nohana, Shimmer, I—"

"Don't," cried Nohana. "If you say it, I don't think I can bear it. Just...just go. Just go, Ayvy, Pol."

She closed her eyes. She heard the door open, and close again. When she looked, Ayvy and Pol were gone.

Bumping into walls and jambs, she ran to her bedroom, and fell to her knees beside her bed. She leaned over the edge of it. Her hand found a pillow, and dragged it closer so that she might rest her face on it. Sobbing uncontrollably now, she scarcely recognized the soft sound of footsteps approaching. She felt Shimmer and Osmares kneel down, one on either side of her. Both bodies shook with grief. Nohana said nothing. For the moment, words eluded her. Together, the three wept.

At last, exhausted of tears, Nohana straightened, and wiped her eyes. Her face felt warm, and she knew it was red now. She had enough left to turn and sit on the edge of the bed. Enough to draw Shimmer and Osmares up beside her. Enough to put her arms around them.

"What will happen to us now?" worried her little sister.

Nohana shook her head; she had given no thought as to what would happen to them. But she knew what they were going to do, even if at the moment she did not know how they were going to do it.

When she spoke, her voice was a bugle, her martial tone mustering the troops. "Right, then," she said. "We're going to war."

www.ingramcontent.com/pod-product-compliance
Lightning Source LLC
LaVergne TN
LVHW012018060526
838201LV00061B/4358